Love is
a time of enchantment:
in it all days are fair and all fields
green. Youth is blest by it,
old age made benign: the eyes of love see
roses blooming in December,
and sunshine through rain. Verily
is the time of true-love
a time of enchantment — and
Oh! how eager is woman
to be bewitched!

THE FAVOURITE SISTER

The story of the downfall of Robert
Devereux, Earl of Essex. The story of
Essex's last five years of triumph and
disaster greatly affected his much loved
sister Penelope Rich. Forced into a
legal marriage but bound by a youthful
betrothal to the man she really loved,
Essex had protected Penelope from
the consequences of a scandal. But
as Essex plunged into the political
quagmire, Penelope's devotion to him
fore-shadowed a terrible climax.

Books by Sheila Bishop
in the Ulverscroft Large Print Series:

A SPEAKING LIKENESS
THE WILDERNESS WALK
THE PARSON'S DAUGHTER
THE SECOND HUSBAND

SHEILA BISHOP

THE FAVOURITE SISTER

Complete and Unabridged

ULVERSCROFT
Leicester

First published in Great Britain in 1967 by
Hurst & Blackett Limited
London

First Large Print Edition
published September 1991

British Library CIP Data

Bishop, Sheila
    The favourite sister. — Large print ed. —
Ulverscroft large print series: romance
I. Title
823.914 [F]

ISBN 0–7089–2493–X

Published by
F. A. Thorpe (Publishing) Ltd.
Anstey, Leicestershire
Set by Words & Graphics Ltd.
Anstey, Leicestershire
Printed and bound in Great Britain by
T. J. Press (Padstow) Ltd., Padstow, Cornwall

Part One

Reflected Glory

August 1596 – December 1597

1

THE sun was halfway down the afternoon sky when a heavy black and yellow coach trundled to a standstill at the southern end of London Bridge. The painted wheels were veiled in dust, the curtains were drawn back to let in the air, and there was a strong smell of hot leather and sweating horses.

Penelope Rich leant out of the window. She could see the narrow chasm of the road running between the two rows of tall houses that spanned the Thames. There was a jostle of people — flat-capped apprentices, merchants' wives, a porter with a load of baskets and a girl crying sweet lavender — threading their way among the carts and waggons that were locked in the usual struggle to get in or out of London by the only bridge.

"Good grief, it grows more intolerable every year." Penelope fanned herself impatiently. She was a vividly beautiful woman of thirty-three, with hair the colour of clouded amber and eyes so dark they were almost black — a breathtaking conjunction. All her qualities were written in her face: generosity and gaiety, with a fiery determination to get her own way. She did not like being kept waiting. "Are we going to sit here till doomsday?"

Her companion said in his pleasantly languid voice, "We might get out and swim."

He crossed his long legs and closed his eyes. He was a tall man with very smooth black hair and an air of polished equanimity that no one could ruffle. He made an excellent foil to Penelope.

Their three-year-old daughter whined, for about the fiftieth time, "Want a drink of water."

"You won't have to wait much longer, moppet. Let me have her now, Mary."

Her mother took the hot and disconsolate little girl from the waiting-gentlewoman who had been trying to keep her amused during the tedious journey.

Perching the small Penny on her knee, so that she could look out at the boats on the river, Penelope said, "I suppose you think I was a fool to bring her, Charles."

Charles Mountjoy opened his eyes and smiled at them with great affection. "My sweet life, I'm only amazed you didn't bring Isabel."

They had left their younger daughter in the care of Robert and Barbara Sidney at Penshurst, where they had been staying when they heard the news which had brought them hurrying back to London.

"I want Penny to be there when her uncle comes home in triumph. It's a day she ought to remember all her life. The conqueror of Cadiz — think of it!"

"I do think of it," said Mountjoy. "Continually."

He had hoped to go on that great adventure with the Earl of Essex, who was Penelope's brother and his closest friend, but at the last moment the Queen had kept him behind, saying that she must have some able-bodied men left at home. The campaign had been a dazzling success, and of a very precious kind. For nine years the English had lived under the constant threat of a Spanish invasion. Three separate armadas had been equipped to destroy them, and there might yet be others; it was dispiriting

5

to go on fighting a defensive war for ever. This summer, at last, they had managed to take the attack right into enemy territory, sinking the best part of the Spanish navy and capturing the great city of Cadiz.

News of the victory had reached England at the end of July. Essex's flagship, *Due Repulse*, had put into Plymouth on the 8th August, and he was expected in London this evening.

The Londoners would give a rapturous welcome to the young Lord General, who was already the most popular man in the kingdom. At this very moment a group of people, passing the coach, recognised Penelope.

"Look there, do you see who it is? Lady Rich, the great Earl's sister."

Penelope glowed with pleasure. Ever since she was eighteen she had been stared at wherever she went, famous as a beauty in her own right, as the Queen's cousin, and as the divine Stella, the heroine of Sir Philip Sidney's sonnets. Lately there had been a new claim to celebrity which she valued more than all the rest: she was the great Earl's sister.

The coach gave a sudden lurch forward, the way was clear, and they were lumbering across London Bridge.

Once over the river, they turned left, jolting along the roughly paved City streets. Peaked gables leaned towards them on either side, dangling shop-signs brushed the roof of the coach. Past St. Paul's and into Fleet Street.

"I grant you Penny won't understand what's happening," said Penelope, "but she'll be able to look back when she's older. I wish . . ."

She broke off. Mountjoy completed the sentence for her. "You wish the other children were here."

"Yes. Well, it can't be helped."

Now they were in the Strand, where the great mansions of the nobility stood in their walled grounds, each with a garden stretching down to a private landing-stage on the river. The coachman drew in his horses and turned them dexterously through an archway into the wide forecourt of Essex House.

A cohort of liveried servants ushered the visitors indoors, and one of the gentlemen of the household said that the

Countess was upstairs in the west gallery. Penny edged close to her father and held his hand. Penelope shook out the creases of her sweeping green skirt. Behind the rigid frame of her stomacher her body was supple and gracefully curved. No stranger would have guessed that she was expecting her eighth child.

Their guide led them ceremoniously up the oak staircase, flourished open a door and announced, "Lady Rich and Lord Mountjoy."

"My dear Penelope!" Frances Essex came forward to greet her sister-in-law. She too was a very pretty woman, in quite a different style: dark and slight and gentle. "I'm so glad — I was certain you would come. What a happy day it is for us all."

There were various other people in the gallery. A childish voice piped up excitedly, "It's my mother!" and a horde of young creatures surrounded Penelope, all talking and exclaiming.

"We persuaded my father to bring us up from Leez ... we wanted to see the processions ... we had a bonfire to celebrate the victory ... the church

8

bells ringing for miles around ... Oh, and you've got Penny ... Where's Bel? Is she here too?"

Penelope was laughing and trying to hug them all at once.

There were actually five of them: Letty and Essex Rich, two exuberant girls of twelve and ten, and three boys, the nine-year-old Robert, and the little ones, Harry and Charles.

On the other side of the gallery stood a stocky, bull-necked man wearing a purple doublet, his small eyes dull as pebbles in a coarse, bad-tempered face. Over the heads of their children Lord Rich stared at the woman who was still his legal wife.

She addressed him with composure. "Well, Rich. How did you leave matters at Leez? Is it a good harvest?"

"I wonder you trouble to ask. The corn could rot in the fields for all the difference it would make to you."

That grudging rancour had hurt her for years before she had ever given him a proper excuse for it. Now she was merely indifferent.

Mountjoy remained beside her, looking supercilious, his face a careful mask for all those feelings which he must never express.

He felt a tug at his sleeve. His godson and namesake, Charles Rich, was gazing up at him, hopefully.

"My lord, will you take me to see the lions at the Tower? You promised, last time we were in London."

Mountjoy hesitated, glancing at Penelope.

"We'll have to see," she said. "It depends on your father."

Charles was only five. He had not yet solved the mysterious equation of his family life.

"Which father?" he enquired with disastrous innocence.

There followed one of those glacial pauses in which no one could think of a single thing to say. The silence was itself more articulate than any comment. Rich glared his dumb resentment. Mountjoy continued to look down his nose. Penelope seemed less affected than either of them. Her eyebrows lifted slightly, but she showed no real concern. It was Frances and the twelve-year-old Letty who blushed for her. Penelope had fought such a hard battle, and for such high stakes, that she could no longer afford to be squeamish. She told her son, quite calmly, that he mustn't ask so many questions, and turned to a man who had risen from his chair by the window and was leaning stiffly on a wooden crutch.

"Mr. Bacon, how is your leg? I hope the pain is easier."

The awkward moment had passed, everything again became ordinary.

One little girl of eleven had been listening with a particular curiosity. She was Elizabeth Sidney, Lady Essex's daughter by her marriage to Sir Philip Sidney, who had died of his wounds after the Battle of Zutphen in 1586. She knew that many years ago, before he married her mother, her father had been deeply in love with Lady Rich. He had told the story of their tragic love in his wonderful sonnet-sequence *Astrophel and Stella*. Elizabeth had read the book surreptitiously, when she was too young to understand it, hungry for details about the father she could not remember. Now she was old enough to have grasped the main facts, if not all the implications. She knew that her father had tried to make Penelope his mistress, and she, loving him in return, had sent him away because she refused to betray her husband or her conscience. Yet here she was, living in sin more or less openly with Lord Mountjoy. Penny and Isabel were his bastards, and everyone knew it. In spite of this, Elizabeth's mother always seemed delighted to see Lady Rich, though she herself was exceptionally pious and strict over questions of right and wrong. It was very strange.

Mountjoy and Rich had sheathed their mutual dislike and were discussing politics. They were well used to the situation. Both belonging to the inner ring of Essex's privileged followers, they had to rub along together as best they could. They were talking to the brilliant and delicate Anthony Bacon, who lived at Essex House and supervised his patron's foreign intelligence service, with its network of correspondents all over Europe: a private undertaking which the Queen relied on as though it was a Government department.

The Rich boys were playing a noisy game with their cousin Robert Hereford,

Essex's son and heir. The girls were gossiping to Penelope.

Frances Essex wandered into the small closet where she wrote her letters. The table was heaped with papers, a flood of unanswered congratulations. She could not attend to them today. Her husband had been away for two and a half months, and now that the danger was over and he was coming back to her, this last afternoon seemed the longest of them all.

She glanced through the doorway into the gallery, and saw her daughter sitting on a cushion, apparently bewitched by Penelope.

"Bess!"

Elizabeth got up reluctantly and came to her.

"Did you want me, madam?"

"Not for any great purpose, sweetheart. But I think you should let the Riches have their mother to themselves for a while."

"Oh." Elizabeth stood on one foot, cogitating. "If I ask you a question, you won't be angry?"

"I don't suppose so. Hadn't you better ask and find out?"

"It's about Lady Rich and Lord Mountjoy — don't you *mind*?"

Frances surveyed her daughter thoughtfully. This had been bound to crop up sooner or later.

"We ought not to condemn others . . . "

"Oh, I don't condemn them," Elizabeth assured her blithely. "But I thought you might. You always say that it's wrong to condone sin."

"Things are not always what they seem. In this case there are certain reasons . . . "

"Does my stepfather compel you to receive her? Because she is his favourite sister?"

"My dear Bess, do you take your stepfather for a tyrant?"

"No," said Elizabeth, who adored him. "But he can twist you round his little finger."

She had heard the servants say that. Frances smiled. It was a fair assumption; no man had ever twisted more skilfully than her beloved Robin. However, on this subject she had made up her own mind.

"I think it's time I told you the true facts." Quietly, she closed the door into the gallery. "Penelope first fell in love

14

with Mountjoy when she was a very young girl. They were secretly betrothed."

"Like Romeo and Juliet."

"She was a little older than Juliet; they were both sixteen. Mind you, he wasn't a lord in those days — he was simply Charles Blount, a younger son with no prospects, serving in the household of her stepfather, Lord Leicester. They were found out, and of course her family wouldn't allow Essex's sister to make such an unequal match; Charles was packed off to Oxford, their letters were intercepted, and that seemed to be the end of it. Two years later she was most unwillingly persuaded into marrying Lord Rich. They say she wept and protested at the actual wedding. If Essex had been older, he might have stopped the match; he was only fourteen and had no say in the matter. I am afraid she was unhappy with Rich, right from the start."

"Was that when my father wrote her those sonnets?"

"Yes. But that's another story . . . In the meantime, Charles was beginning to make his way in the world. He was knighted at Zutphen, the day your father

15

was mortally wounded, and at Court he gained the support and approval of the Queen. He and Essex became close friends, they were always in each other's company, and generally Penelope was there too. By now Sir Charles was heir to the Mountjoy barony, and a rising man, so it seemed strange he did not marry. One day Penelope discovered the reason. He had made a great study of theology, and he had decided, as a result of all his reading, that the promises he and Penelope had exchanged when they were sixteen amounted to a marriage by declaration, so that they were bound to each other in the sight of God. He felt that he could never marry anyone else so long as she lived."

"You mean that Sir Charles had been her husband all along, and not Lord Rich?"

"That is what he thought."

"But the children — are they illegitimate? Do they know?"

"I don't think so. Bess, you must never repeat any of this. I am trusting you to keep a secret, although you are so young, because I don't want you to

16

grow up thinking that all scandals are a laughing matter and every woman can behave as badly as she pleases. This is a very special case."

"I won't breathe a word. What did she do — after Sir Charles had told her?"

"At the time, nothing. At first she didn't believe him. After all, she and Rich had been married in church, and she didn't want to do anything that would hurt the children. Sir Charles wasn't threatening her; he was ready to keep his mouth shut if that was what she wanted. They agreed never to speak of the matter again. However, it must have made a difference. After three years they admitted that they had fallen in love with each other for the second time. At this point they hoped to get her marriage to Rich declared invalid, on account of her earlier contract to Sir Charles. They consulted Francis Bacon, and he told them they didn't stand a chance, they had no evidence and no witnesses to prove their claim. So it wasn't worth trying. But they could not face another separation, and a few months later Penelope found she was going to

17

have a child. They were in great trouble; if Rich had brought an action for divorce, Penelope would have become an outcast and Sir Charles's career might have been ruined. Luckily your stepfather was by then such a power in the State that he was able to protect them. He persuaded both Rich and the Queen to accept the situation with complaisance. No one else could have done it."

"Penelope is bound to spend some months of every year on Lord Rich's estate at Leez, or at his town mansion in the Bow Road; they attend all the great court functions together, and he hasn't publicly disowned her two youngest children. The greater part of the time she lives apart from Rich, but not under the same roof as Lord Mountjoy. As you know, they both have their London houses."

Conveniently close; Mountjoy lived in Holborn, and Penelope had a pretty little house in the old monastic precincts of St. Bartholomew's Priory.

Bess thought dreamily that it was the most wonderful love story she had ever heard, as good as anything in Malory: Tristram and Isolde, or

Lancelot and Guinevere. Better, because these two lovers, while braving the world's condemnation, knew themselves to be honestly married in the sight of God. Though it seemed very strange that they could have achieved this without a proper wedding in church.

"Do you believe that they are married?" she asked her mother.

Frances Essex hesitated. She was certain that Charles Mountjoy believed it. Born a Catholic, he had sheered away from the old religion to an extreme form of Protestantism which granted each man a free approach to God through his own conscience, without intervention from the priesthood. Frances was the daughter of the great puritan Secretary of State, Sir Francis Walsingham; she could respect such opinions, but she was not sure how far she agreed with them when it came to the validity of a marriage that was simply an exchange of promises without any formal ceremony. She was still less certain what Penelope thought. She had sometimes felt that the vital and entrancing Penelope had been swept along on the tide of events, believing what she needed to believe. It was a family failing.

Frances saw that her daughter was still waiting, as though expecting a pronouncement from the Delphic oracle. And then she was saved from answering, because Mr. Reynolds, her husband's principal secretary, arrived to say that his lordship's party was approaching the house — they could hear the sound of cheering all along the Strand. Everything else was forgotten.

The family flocked down into the forecourt, to be tantalised by a long delay, as the exciting swell of noise grew slowly but invisibly nearer in the road outside. All they could see through the gate was the back of a row of citizens, tightly packed for a glimpse of the returning hero. At last the shouts rose to a climax, the people in the archway scuttled aside, and a small troop of horsemen trotted into the yard. The man at their head was tall and slender, beautifully proportioned. He wore plain military dress, with a white plume in the broad-brimmed hat which he swept off in a salute to the party by the door. They could see him clearly now: his splendidly patrician profile, finely-cut as a cameo, the high-bridged nose, the sensuous mouth. His hair was a dark tawny-brown, but he had a small red beard.

He rode right up to them and swung himself out of the saddle.

"Here we are, at long last!" He was laughing, and his wonderful dark eyes seemed to be dancing with light. "Getting into my own house is harder work than taking Cadiz. Well, sweetheart, are you glad to see your storm-tossed mariner?"

He held out his hands to his wife.

"My lord, you are most truly welcome."

Frances advanced stiffly. Her public manner was always very reserved. Essex was never one to stand on ceremony. He took her in his arms and kissed her mouth, murmuring, "Frank, dear Frank," as though they were quite alone.

Robert Hereford was clamouring for attention. "I want to hear about your battle."

"All in due time, sparrow. Have you been good while I was gone? Oh, what a curmudgeonly question — I shouldn't have asked. Bess, my treasure, I am sure you have been a paragon."

Having greeted his son and stepdaughter, Essex immediately turned to Penelope. "I hoped I'd find you here."

"Wild horses wouldn't have kept me away." She embraced her brother, and then stood back to scrutinise him with a mixture of affection and amusement. "Robin, why didn't you warn us? I never thought you'd come home with a beard."

"It was confoundedly troublesome shaving at sea." He rubbed his chin. "Do you like it? Shall I keep it?"

"That's for Frank to decide."

In fact it was probably his Queen, not his wife, who would settle the fate of the new beard. Penelope was not certain about it; she disliked beards as a rule. Charles was clean-shaven, and under orders to remain so. But it was diverting to find that Robin's beard was red, the exact colour his hair had been when he was a little boy. She did not think this sisterly comparison would be well received. It surprised her, these days, to remember that she had rocked her brother in his cradle. This tall young general had outstripped her in every direction. He was only twenty-nine; he had been the

Queen's principal favourite since he was nineteen.

When they sat down to supper, Penelope was placed between Essex and their step-father, Sir Christopher Blount, who had married their mother, a formidable beauty, in rather disgraceful circumstances just after the death of her second husband, the famous Earl of Leicester. Kit Blount was Charles Mountjoy's cousin; he was eighteen years younger than his wife and not much older than his stepchildren. Penelope had a low opinion of his private character, but he was a brave and competent soldier. He had been at Cadiz with Essex, and was full of his praises.

"I wish you could have seen him, Pen, on the deck of *Due Repulse*, as we sailed into Cadiz harbour through the narrow strait under Fort Puntal, with the Spanish guns loosing off at us; I was afraid for my life. His lordship never batted an eyelid."

"It must have been like walking into a trap. You tried to land outside the harbour, didn't you, at first? On the open beaches?"

"That's what Howard wanted, but the seas are too rough on that coast, we'd never have got the men ashore. Essex kept telling him so, but Howard wouldn't listen. Thought he was still sinking the Armada, I suppose. He's too old and obstinate."

The expedition had been sent out with a divided authority; Essex was to be in sole command once they landed, but his cousin Howard of Effingham, the veteran Lord Admiral, was in charge of the sea operation.

"I thought he was going to drown my army before we started," Essex was saying across the table to Charles. "I couldn't make him see sense. And then who should come to my aid, of all people but Ralegh."

"You and Ralegh made an unexpected alliance."

The Queen's two favourites had been at daggers drawn for years.

"He's a different man at sea," said Essex. "We found we liked each other very well. A pity he was wounded so early in the engagement. But he's none the worse for it now."

24

He went on talking about the campaign, his listeners hanging on every detail. They already knew the brief outline, from the accounts that had been sent home with the first report of the victory.

Directly the English ships had penetrated the harbour, they were embroiled in a desperate battle at close quarters, which ended in the virtual destruction of the Spanish fleet. The great galleons, the 'Apostles', burst into flames, men poured into the sea in a carnage of blood and panic, and the Lord General, now in control, made ready for the land attack.

The walled city of Cadiz was three miles from the port. An orthodox commander would have waited overnight while his whole army disembarked. Essex had already had a hard day's fighting, but he set off at once, with only a thousand men, on a lightning forced march across the dunes in the intolerable heat of late afternoon. The surprise was completely successful. The Spaniards who came out to meet them were demoralised and soon routed. Essex scaled the walls at the head of his men. Barely fifty of the toughest were still managing to keep up with him when he fought his way into the Market Place. But the rest were close behind, the Spanish resistance broke, and by dusk the city was at the mercy of the English general. It was the most spectacular exploit of the entire war.

The citizens had waited in terror for the vengeance of the heretics. They knew what to expect, they knew what their own people had done at Antwerp. Gradually fear gave way to astonishment. There was no sickening orgy of murder and rape, no drunken violence, no wholesale robbery. The city was later pillaged, according to the custom of war, but with an orderly moderation. All women and children were protected, ladies allowed to keep their jewels, nuns shepherded to safety by the English officers. The churches were declared inviolate, not one Protestant hand was laid on their sacred images, and when distinguished prelates were brought before the Lord General, they found he simply wanted to discuss theology.

"And mightily astounded they were at his learning," said Kit Blount, laughing. He was a Catholic himself, though not a very good one.

Essex, though an extreme Protestant, respected all forms of religion, and held the extraordinary view that men should be left free to worship as they chose.

He was indeed a man of curious contradictions: a great lord who liked mingling with the common people, a successful courtier who despised luxury and affectation, a born soldier who enjoyed fighting but detested brutality.

The Spaniards must have been bewildered by their conqueror, after all they had heard about the godless Northern barbarians. It was quite obvious that the Count, as they called him, was not only a cultivated European nobleman but also a chivalrous and devout Christian. King Philip's subjects were already tiring of their war against the English. Anthony Bacon, the leading student of foreign affairs, had remarked to Penelope earlier that Essex's conduct after the victory might have had as important an effect as the victory itself.

Anthony was sitting at the corner of the table, his lame leg propped on a low stool. His younger brother Francis was here too. This amazingly gifted pair were the nephews of William Cecil, Lord Burleigh, the Lord Treasurer, who might have been expected to help them on in their careers. But Burleigh was jealous of his clever nephews: he did not want them to outshine his own ewe lamb, his hunchback son Robert. So they had found a more generous patron in Essex, who was warmly attached to them both.

Apart from the Bacons, it was a family gathering. Penelope caught Charles's eye across the table, and they exchanged a secret, confiding smile. Frank was sitting on the other side of her husband. She looked beautiful and serene.

Rich, sipping his claret, considered the aspect of the campaign that interested him most.

"It was unfortunate you weren't able to capture their merchant fleet."

Trust Rich to see it all in terms of profit and loss. But he was quite right — it was unfortunate.

"Howard's fault again," said Essex. "While I was fully occupied in the town, his lordship sat on his backside in the port and let Medina Sidonia sink all that rich cargo of pepper and spices to prevent our laying hands on it. And then the treasure fleet from the Indies never arrived, though it was weeks overdue. I wanted to stay out there and lie in wait for it. In fact, I wanted to garrison Cadiz and hold it for the Crown, as we used to hold Calais. But no! Howard and the Council of War were all against me. So we came home. The best thing I brought back with me was a great library of books that I took from a Spanish bishop; I think I'll give them to Tom Bodley, he can set them in order. Which reminds me, has that appointment been confirmed yet?"

There was a short silence. At the time Essex went abroad the Queen had been about to appoint a new Secretary of State. It was in some ways the most influential post in the country. Essex had been pressing the claims of his friend Thomas Bodley; he thought he had convinced her. Now someone would have to disillusion him.

It was Francis Bacon who delivered the blow, his precise lawyer's voice seemed designed to break bad news with exemplary detachment.

"I am afraid your lordship will be disappointed. Her Majesty has given the office to my cousin Robert."

"My God, that's too much! Robert Cecil! His father's doing, of course. I might have known how it would be. The moment my back was turned, they were sniffing round after what they could get, that precious pair. Can I never leave the Court? Am I supposed to be in two places at once? What's the use of winning battles overseas, if everything I've fought for is going to be steadily undermined at Whitehall?"

He had gone pale with anger beneath his Spanish sunburn, and the flexible mouth was taut and thin. Frances laid a hand on his wrist.

"Robin, don't brood over it tonight. You are tired; it won't seem so bad in the morning."

She dreaded his political quarrels, and he knew it. He was not usually amenable to restraint, but he had missed his wife very much, and at this moment he would do anything she wanted.

"Don't fret, Frank," he said gently. "I'm not going to act any tragedies. I'm home with my family, that's the main thing. And soon we'll go to Wanstead. Let the devil fly away with the Cecils."

2

"SO my standard has flown in triumph from the ramparts of a Spanish citadel." The magic, unmistakeable voice was as resonant as a lute-string, and as expressive; the pride in it quivered with undertones of irony. "I wonder what my royal brother-in-law said when they told him."

That voice was the Queen's last remaining beauty. Everything else was a travesty. She was sixty-three years old, and racked by the pain of a chronic ulcer in her leg. Her entire life had been a struggle for survival. But the mask painted on her lean, aquiline face was a work of art, and her orange wig was dressed in the latest fashion. Her pale yellow dress and low-cut bodice would have looked exquisite on a young girl.

She smiled at her favourite and patted his hand. "You've been a great traveller on my behalf, Robin. The Low Countries, Portugal, France — now Spain. And I have never left England."

"That would be inconceivable, madam. The heart can't leave the body. This Eden would wither into a wilderness without Your Majesty."

It was extraordinary, thought Penelope, how Robin could bring out such a remark as though he meant it. On second thoughts, he was such a bad liar that the note of conviction was almost certainly sincere. Which was equally extraordinary. As a hero-worshipping boy he had been dazzled into accepting Elizabeth as the goddess of wisdom — while observing the convention that she must always be treated as the goddess of love. By now he no longer mistook her for either, yet she still cast a spell over him.

"As for my travels," he was saying, "I have gone always as your swordbearer. I want to make you mistress of the seas, which is the kind of greatness that the Queen of an island should aspire to."

Was this the key to the riddle? That he directed towards her the passionate love he felt for England? Not entirely. Robin was an idealist, but he was very dependent on the give-and-take of human affection.

There was an odd, tough, wayward affinity between those two; each seemed to enjoy in the other's company something that neither could find elsewhere.

They were walking under the trees in the park at Greenwich, followed by a small and select party of courtiers. Robin squired the Queen protectively, shortening his steps to suit her, and stooping a little from his great height. He was very fine today: his peacock blue doublet had immense padded sleeves and a narrow waist above the jewelled buckle of his belt. His long legs were immaculate in carnation silk stockings. This, his sister knew, must be due to the frantic efforts of his gentlemen-in-waiting, for Robin was not interested in clothes and hardly noticed what he was wearing. He had become a courtier by accident, and frequently broke the rules. Though a superb athlete, he disliked dancing and could never remember the steps, a fault the Queen would not have tolerated in any other favourite; Robin's ineptitude merely amused her. It was one of the many concessions she made to the fascinating cousin who was thirty-four years younger than herself.

They had arrived at a stone seat overlooking the river. Servants hurried forward with cushions. The Queen sat down and made a slight gesture to Robin, permitting him to sit on the grass at her feet. A stool was produced for old Lord Burleigh. Howard of Effingham, the Lord Admiral, stood four-square, indifferent to his comfort. He was a tall man of sixty-two, active and alert, his white hair cropped short. Sir Robert Cecil, the new Secretary of State, stood beside his father. He was tragically deformed, one shoulder twisted up behind his neck in a great hump. He had a penetrating wit, and could be very entertaining.

Penelope effaced herself with the two attendant maids of honour who hovered behind the Queen. She had an official post as a woman of the bedchamber; she was not on duty, owing to her pregnancy, but the Queen had probably forgotten that, and Penelope had wormed her way into this al fresco audience by making herself useful; she was carrying Her Majesty's gloves and fan.

When the military success had been

thoroughly discussed, the Queen intro-
duced a less agreeable topic. "Let us
come to matters of accountancy. When I
sanctioned this expedition, you promised
to make me not only glorious but rich.
You promised me the year's harvest of
bullion from the Indies."

"The treasure fleet was late. If I had
been allowed to stay out there . . . "

"You could not cruise around the high
seas indefinitely. You had your orders."

"I believe the merchant fleet was already
in port," remarked the Lord Treasurer.
With his heavy features and grey beard,
Burleigh looked rather like a benevolent
sheep. This was deceptive. He was a very
crafty old gentleman indeed. He knew
perfectly well what had happened to the
merchant fleet, and so did the Queen.

Essex said nothing. He was exasperated
with the Lord Admiral for having let the
Spaniards destroy the precious cargo of
spices, but they were good friends: he
was not going to abuse Howard in front
of the Cecils.

The Queen dismissed the merchant
fleet. "No use crying over spilt milk.
There still remains the booty you captured

in the city, and that must have come to a goodly total. How great is my share?"

The two commanders exchanged glances. This was a most embarrassing question. It was true that the spoils had been enormous, but most of them had mysteriously vanished on the voyage home. An epidemic of corruption had run through every ship in the fleet, no one seemed able or willing to protect government property. Captains and officers, soldiers and seamen — they had all grabbed what they could get in a frenzy of greed.

Essex and Howard explained this as tactfully as they could. Both scrupulously honest, they had taken nothing beyond their due, but they knew they vere going to get the blame.

The Queen listened with growing displeasure and incredulity, twisting the rings on her narrow, avaricious hands.

"Is this how you carry out your stewardship? I would not have believed it possible. My subjects are allowed to rob me with impunity while the Lord General and the Lord Admiral stand back and do nothing! I wonder you have the temerity to come and tell me such a story."

Not trusting Essex to speak, Howard said: "It is a matter of deep regret to us both, madam. But there was nothing we could do. By the time we knew what was happening, it was too late to stop it."

"That is a very curious admission," said Robert Cecil.

Howard rounded on him. "What do you mean by that, Mr. Secretary? Are you suggesting that Lord Essex and I are engaged in a treasonable fraud?"

"I should not dream of making such a base accusation against your lordships. I am merely surprised that you did not foresee the pilfering and take steps to prevent it."

In other words, if you are not knaves, you must be a pair of incompetent fools. Cecil had scored his point.

The four men glared at each other across the barrier of divergent policies that always divided them. Basically they all wanted the same thing: the integrity of England as a free sovereign state. None of them wished to see their country crushed into a servile dependency of the great Spanish Empire. But while

Essex and Howard thought they could only safeguard their liberty by going on with the war, the Cecils believed the real danger was over. They would like a negotiated peace, apparently convinced that the Spaniards would abide by the terms and leave England alone to build up her national prosperity.

The Queen's attitude was less definite. In the threat of attack she was as brave as an Amazon, and she had no illusions about her brother-in-law and lifelong enemy, Philip of Spain, but she hated war as much as she hated waste. It suited the Cecils to go on quietly insisting that the Cadiz Expedition had cost a great deal of money and brought her nothing in return but empty glory.

They played this tune very successfully for the next fortnight. The Queen was in a most irritable frame of mind. She doted on Essex, and was delighted to have him back, but she could not overlook the loss of all that Spanish plunder. Her favourites were allowed no licence to make mistakes in their capacity as public servants, which was a sound enough principle — if only she had not been so ignorant and illiberal about the difficulties of her generals. And so grasping. Victories meant nothing to her unless they could be translated into the solid language of pounds, shillings and pence. Essex had won a fortune for her and then let it slip through his fingers. She could not forget that and she nagged him incessantly.

Matters were not improved by Sir Walter Ralegh, who had quickly reverted to his usual habit of self-aggrandizement, and was spreading it about that he was responsible for the victory; Essex had accomplished nothing.

Essex felt thoroughly ill-used, and went to Court as little as possible. In the world outside it was different, and he was fully compensated by the adoration of the English people. They loved him already for his good looks and engaging manners; now he was a national hero. He had only to put a foot out of doors for the Londoners to flock round, calling down blessings on his name, holding up their children to see him. Essex House was filled with friends and admirers from morning to night, and Penelope got a good deal of attention as the Earl's favourite sister.

She constantly rejected this title, saying it was unjust to their other sister, Dorothy Northumberland. He was extremely fond of her too. The four Devereux had been a most united family. Now there were just the three of them; their younger brother Walter had been killed fighting under Robin's command, six years ago in France.

Still, it was true that Penelope and Robin had always been specially close, and she was very proud of him now. She had never known anything like the excitement of being with him in London this autumn, engulfed in a tremendous wave of emotion as the crowds surged round their darling.

"He's getting too popular for his own good," said Francis Bacon.

It was the kind of tiresome pessimism one might expect from him, thought Penelope. They were in the high, panelled chamber at Essex House that Robin used for conferences. She answered the lawyer with a touch of impatience.

"Can any man be too popular?"

41

"Certainly, madam. If that man is a subject and his sovereign a Tudor."

Anthony Bacon limped to the table with a sheaf of papers.

"His lordship has one rare distinction," he remarked. "He is the only royal favourite in the whole of our history who has not been detested by the common people."

"And another distinction that I find more disturbing," retorted his brother. "He is the only person in the thirty-eight years of Her Majesty's reign who has drawn a fraction of the people's regard away from herself."

So Francis thought the Queen was jealous.

The door swung open and Robin came in, with his quick, stooping stride.

"Good morning, Pen. No need to ask how you are; you always contrive to look so handsome when you're breeding. Mr. Bacon, how often have I told you not to stand up when I come into a room? If you wish to pay some sort of tribute to my authority, you might at least attend to what I say."

The cripple smiled, and subsided into

his chair. His master then set about arranging his footstool. Although Anthony Bacon was actually one of his paid servants, Robin invariably treated him with a respect that was rather touching.

The room was filling up. Mountjoy and Rich had come in with the Earl of Southampton. Harry Southampton was a beautiful young man who wore his hair rather too long; he had a great deal of charm but was inclined to be dramatic and flamboyant. He was a complete contrast to Charles Mountjoy, whose austere elegance and cool manner presented a surface of repose, suggesting hidden depths, that was far more arresting.

Two of Robin's five secretaries were in attendance. He sat down at the table, sorting through his letters at a prodigious rate.

"Council of Wales, Inns of Court, University of Cambridge — you can deal with that one, Cuffe. (Make yourselves at ease, my lords, I shall soon be done.) What's this? A petition regarding the sad plight of the Puritans. We'd better invite the Archbishop to dinner next week ... Reynolds, see if you can find Lady Essex. Oh, there you are, my love."

Frank had just joined them. Penelope noted how much it improved her to have a little colour in her cheeks, she was inclined to be too pale. Frank was happy, that was the secret. She did not have an easy marriage. Robin loved her very much, but he was a flagrantly unfaithful husband. However, since coming home from Cadiz on a high tide of exaltation, he had made a solemn vow to reform, and they were living in a golden age of hope and affection.

She took her place beside him, the others assembled in a circle. Robin leant back, absently playing with a crystal paperweight, as he began to talk about affairs of state. His swift, far-reaching mind leapt from one point to the next, he uncovered the connection between them, analysing as he went. It was a remarkably versatile performance. They listened in silent concentration. This was no idle discourse; they were all there to share information, debate and take their orders, for this was the inner conclave of the Essex faction. The three noblemen:

Mountjoy and Southampton, his closest friends, and Rich, his brother-in-law, who knew a great deal about finance. The Bacon brothers, reputed to be the cleverest men in the kingdom. Anthony Bacon was the presiding genius of Essex's foreign intelligence service. The two women: Frances worked with Anthony on the foreign reports — she was not Walsingham's daughter for nothing. And Penelope had a special role. For some years now, under her brother's direction, she had been carrying on a secret correspondence with the King of Scots, the rightful heir to the throne, who could never persuade the Queen to acknowledge him, and wanted to be sure that her most powerful subject would support his claim.

The two secretaries, Reynolds and Cuffe, were busy making notes. They were both in their master's confidence and both extremely able. There were enough brains in that room to furnish a second Privy Council. In a sense, that was what it was.

Ever since he was nineteen, the Queen had been training Essex to be a statesman.

Now that she had succeeded, he was not content to attend the Council as a mere figurehead, to play second fiddle to Burleigh or condone the suicidal folly of making peace with Spain. So he was taking steps to strengthen his position. He knew that knowledge meant power, just as military success meant popularity. He was very well fitted to acquire both.

They were discussing the troubles in Ireland when there was a tentative rap on the door, and one of the junior secretaries came in with a letter.

"From your lordship's agent at Plymouth. The courier says that the contents are most urgent."

Robin slit the seal and began to read. After a minute he threw the letter down in disgust.

"Of all the confounded pieces of bad luck. It's enough to make a man weep."

"What's happened?" asked Frank.

"One of our privateers captured a Spanish barque off Finisterre, and got from her all the news of the coast. The treasure fleet sailed into Cadiz two days after we left."

There was an outburst of commiseration,

as everyone thought of the great prize, the galleons loaded down with silver that the English invaders had missed by such a narrow margin. What a difference it would have made, to the depleted treasury; to Robin himself, head over ears in debt; to the welcome he had received from the Queen.

"How angry she's going to be," he said.

"Yes, my dear lord," said Charles in his calm way. "But not with you."

Robin looked at him and laughed. "You're right, Charles. That's a measure of consolation. I think I must present myself immediately at the Palace."

The Queen was furious — but not with Robin. He alone was exonerated. Everyone else was caught up in the whirlwind. She was angry with Howard and Ralegh for dragging Essex home (even though they had simply obeyed her orders). She was far more angry with Burleigh for persuading her to give those orders; she said it was all his fault that Essex hadn't been able to capture the treasure, and he had been intriguing against the Earl ever since. She had been unkind to Robin and she knew it, so she said she would never forgive the miscreant who had been poisoning her mind.

Burleigh had endured the Queen's temper for thirty-eight years, but now, at seventy-six, this was more than he could bear. He was extremely devoted to her, and his condition was pitiful. He wrote Essex a most abject letter of apology, threw himself on his mercy and begged him to intercede with the Queen.

All his life Essex had been intermittently plagued by Burleigh, his former guardian, who had scolded him when he was a boy and obstructed him ever since, but he was moved to compassion by the old man's distress. He was too generous to go on kicking an opponent once he was down. (Politically, this was a disadvantage, though he would never admit it.) He coaxed the Queen out of her rancour and peace was restored.

Things were going so well for him that Robin was now in a mood of charity with all men. One day in November, when Frank was visiting her mother, he asked Penelope to act as his hostess at a small supper-party; he was entertaining two of his great friends. She agreed, and asked who they were. When he told her, she laughed, her black eyes sparkling.

"Robin! You don't mean it?"

"Why not? Sir Robert Cecil and Sir Walter Ralegh are two of my very great friends these days and so I mean to keep them."

And with that unexpected trio she sat down to supper in Robin's winter parlour, the tall spires of candlelight multiplied in the burnished curves of the plate, and the blues and greens of the arras, outside the ring of brightness, merging together like the dim depths of a forest.

Penelope was wearing a wide-sleeved robe of chestnut velvet, with a necklace or clustered orient pearls swinging to her waist. Though her baby was due in two months' time, she could still look magnificent, and she saw that Ralegh thought so, studying her with his strange, enigmatic eyes.

Whatever might be said of Ralegh, he was one of those people whose physical presence had an impact on the most grudging observer. She had once thought he must have Italian blood, but Charles said he was partly Cornish. The Cornish pirate.

They were on their guard with each other, and began a highly artificial exchange about books. Presently she told him she had been reading his *Discovery of Guiana*.

Ralegh gave his short, hard laugh. "Did you know that some of my enemies are saying I never went there? That I invented the whole account while I was skulking at Sherborne?"

"Well, Sir Walter, if you imagined those exotic scenes in the middle of Dorset, you must be an even better writer than I took you for." Then, more seriously, "How spiteful people are, and how obtuse. Why shouldn't you have gone? Sea voyages hold no terrors for you."

"Your ladyship flatters me. I can be as frightened as the next man. Yet I suppose the lust for travel was bred in my bones."

He started to talk of his youth in the West Country, of his half-brother Humphrey Gilbert and his cousin Richard

Grenvile. His affectations dropped from him, he became simple and sincere, an enthusiast. This must be what Robin meant when be said that Ralegh was a different man once you got him aboard a ship.

Robin was listening too. He asked a question, Ralegh answered, and the discussion grew technical. Penelope turned to Robert Cecil.

It was never difficult to find anything to say to him. The smooth-tongued, dwarfish little man could create the delightful impression that he was revealing his confidences to the only other sensible person in the universe. He was drily amusing about the duties of the Secretary of State.

"A Jack of All Trades, madam. This morning, for instance, I spent hounding a seditious printer into the Clink."

"They're a troublesome tribe. What had this one printed?"

"A pamphlet about the succession."

"And what did it say — if it isn't treasonable to ask questions regarding the succession?"

"It's rapidly becoming treasonable even

to mention the succession," retorted Cecil, with a satirical gleam.

That was one of the chief trials that beset them all. The older the Queen grew, the more she resented any reference to the vexed question of who was to come after her. Which was understandable in a way, but it did not satisfy the rising generation who expected to outlive her. What they dreaded most was a civil war as soon as the Queen was dead. Although the King of Scots had the clearest legal claim, he was a foreigner, and so was the Spanish Infanta — she would be the Catholic choice. There was also Lady Arabella Stuart, English by upbringing and the pawn of her ambitious family.

Penelope cracked a piece of marchpane thoughtfully. "At the risk of joining your printer in the Clink, Sir Robert, I must say that I wish the Crown could pass by the fixed laws of inheritance. No one doubts who will succeed to the titles in your family or mine."

"But peerages don't descend through the female line, and neither of us has a foreign candidate in our pedigree. The English are an insular people, not willing to admit the stranger within their gates, not even certain that it would be lawful. And when there is no Prince of Wales, the Sovereign's own choice of an heir has long been held to be paramount." Cecil lowered his voice, forming his words with deliberation. "That's the main thesis of this impertinent pamphlet. That the merest drop of Plantagenet blood might prove sufficient, if Her Majesty were to elect a pure-bred Englishman, a great public servant, to be our future King."

He glanced towards the man at the head of the table.

"Oh no!" said Penelope. "I thought we had done with that story." She looked to see whether Robin had overheard, but he and Ralegh were happily dissecting the shortcomings of the Lord Admiral.

"This pamphlet," she said to Cecil. "Has the Queen read it? Need you tell her? There was a book on the same subject, as you know, two years ago, and my brother was afraid she would think he had inspired it. We do have a remote Plantagenet strain, like most of the old nobility, and we are related to Her Majesty through the Boleyns, but we are not royal, and he is no usurper. He would never try to seize the Crown. In his eyes that would amount to sacrilege."

"I know that, Lady Rich. So does Her Majesty. Don't you remember, when that book was published, how she took his innocence for granted? Yet these wild ideas might inflame his more hotheaded supporters. I thought it wise to give you a hint. I am such a devoted admirer of his lordship, glad to do him any small service."

"I thank you, Sir Robert," said Penelope politely.

Could he be a devoted admirer? Possibly, for he loved the smell of success. He had also been testing her, trying to find out where Robin really stood. She might have fallen into the trap by protesting that he was already pledged to the King of Scots. But the knowledge that he had given such a pledge, even to the rightful heir, would infuriate the Queen. It was an absurd situation.

They were both silent. Their companions had plenty to say to each other. Strictures on the Lord Admiral had led them back to Cadiz and to various episodes on that wonderful day. Robin was reliving the moment on *Due Repulse* when he had seen Ralegh's longboat returning from the flagship. Ralegh had gone to persuade Howard into making a direct attack inside the harbour. As his boat came alongside, he had shouted up to Robin: 'Entramos!' We go in. Borrowing from the enemy's language, like every English soldier since the Crusades.

"Was that when you threw your hat into the sea?" Penelope asked her brother.

Robin smiled. "That's a slander. I never threw my hat into the sea, as Sir Walter will testify. I threw it in the air. It fell into the sea."

"You had better let the legend stick, my lord," said Ralegh. "It has a prodigal ardour that becomes you."

This might have been sardonic, yet Penelope sensed behind the bantering wit an honest regard for his brother-in-arms.

She was very conscious of Cecil, the hunchback who could never share the fellowship of men who had fought side by side in the same engagement. Those others — with their straight bodies and masculine achievements — they had been given all the advantages. To them it was a particular piece of good luck that they were living in the reign of a susceptible woman. Cecil could not even dismiss the favourites as two handsome blockheads, for they were both distinguished poets, both scholars whose wide learning left him plodding behind, the useful little clerk. What was he really feeling? Envy, hatred and malice? If so, she could hardly blame him. But his expression showed nothing so positive. It was detached and curiously calculating. For some reason she was chilled.

Then Robin turned to Cecil with his natural courtesy and drew him into the conversation.

Penelope leant her elbows on the table. Her baby was kicking, and suddenly the weight of her jewels seemed heavy. Very soon she would withdraw. Robin had wanted a hostess to start the evening on a casual note, but presently he would talk to these men alone. She did not know what they would say, only that both the adventurer and the politician wanted an alliance and that would suit his purpose. He was not angling after the Crown.

Her assurances to Cecil had been quite truthful. No need to stress the part he had chosen. A kingmaker. Fate was playing into his hands. The Queen was old; every year that diminished her was bringing her young cousin and favourite towards his zenith. She would lean on him more and more. Until inevitably the end must come. (If it was melancholy, as well as treasonable, to contemplate that end, it was also irreligious to pretend that any earthly prince could reign for ever. And she was nearly old enough to be their grandmother.) They would proclaim the King of Scots, and whether he ascended the throne peaceably, or whether they had to fight for him, it would be Robin who put him there and kept him there. Robin, his principal subject, to whom he must turn for guidance among the bewildering laws and customs of a strange land.

Robin was convinced of the way he had to take. As the servant of an ageing Queen and a foreign King, he would fulfil his own destiny. He would become the actual ruler of England.

3

THE baby was a boy. His parents were enchanted with him, though there was a stab of pain too, for Charles's son should have been the heir to his barony. In the tearful aftermath of child-bearing, from which even she was not immune, Penelope worked herself into a fit of remorse because she had broken the vow she made to Charles sixteen years before and let her family shackle her to Rich. She did not see how Charles could forgive her for having been so wicked.

He comforted her, stroking her bright hair and calling her his Angel. She had not understood, he said, any more than he did at the time, what that vow really entailed.

He never reproached her for placing him in this wretched position where he was judged as an adulterer for going to bed with the woman he regarded as his lawful wife, whom he could possess only in a nebulous kind of half-marriage that was unsanctified by the Church and unrecognised by the State. There had been one solitary moment of bitterness, four years ago, when she had tried to break with him in order to become a Catholic. He had talked her out of that, he was an acute Protestant theologian, and she had let him convince her, though it still weighed on her conscience that they had not been married in church. Surely he had earned some right to claim that what they were doing was justified simply by the way he had always treated her? Charles was the model of what a husband ought to be: patient, loving and faithful.

They called the child Mountjoy, defiantly, giving him for a Christian name the title he could never inherit. Soon Penelope was her buoyant self again; she was too happy to be cast down for long.

In the late spring they went to Wanstead, Robin's country house in Essex. It was a splendid mansion, almost a little palace, of weathered rose brick, built on a stretch of upland at the edge of the Forest of Waltham, with a magnificent view. On a clear day you could see St. Paul's. Yet though it was barely ten miles from the City, Wanstead had an Arcadian seclusion, and Penelope always loved staying there. When she was a girl it had belonged to the Earl of Leicester, who was then their stepfather. After his death it had come to Robin. It was at Wanstead that she and Charles had met when they were both sixteen and exchanged the promises which they had later ratified in the face of so many obstacles.

Robin was in high fettle, because the Queen had given him permission to lead another assault on the enemy this summer. He was talking about his plans one afternoon, as he and Charles and Penelope strolled beside the fishpond that Charles had designed and stocked for him. Charles was a great authority on gardening and a keen fisherman.

"She'll let you come with me this time, Charles. I have her assurance that she won't keep you at home."

Charles was delighted. Penelope was not.

"I can't think why you want to go. You've got plenty to do here; you are Lord

Lieutenant of Hampshire and Captain of Portsmouth . . . "

"That ever I should hear such heresy from a daughter of the house of Devereux! Your womenfolk have been cheering their men into battle ever since the Conquest. What would you think of Frank if she used such arguments to Robert?"

"She wouldn't dare," said Penelope. "And that's a different matter; he was bred to be a soldier, like my father, and he gets so restless that I expect poor Frank is glad to see the back of him. It's like putting the dog out for a run."

"A most poetic fancy," said Robin. "I thank you. What kind of an animal is Charles?"

"Oh, a black cat that sits by the fire and looks wise."

Both men laughed. There was something catlike about Charles, in his air of remoteness, his quiet and graceful elegance, his strong dislike of being uncomfortable. Of course he had seen active service like most men of his generation: she wouldn't have wanted a weakling or a coward. But his talents flowered in another climate; he was a notable patron of the arts, a creator of beautiful gardens, a scholar, a lawyer, a theologian. In time she was sure he would be on the Privy Council, perhaps he would hold one of the great offices of state. There was no incentive for him to hunt for glory on a battlefield.

"That's all very well," said Charles, with a slight note of chagrin. "I may be an indolent popinjay, but I did fight in the Low Countries, and in France ... "

"France! You don't think I have forgotten your exploits on that occasion! Stealing off without Her Majesty's permission, and being brought back like a schoolboy who'd played truant. Yes, and do you recall what she said to you then? That you'd never rest until you got yourself knocked on the head like that inconsiderate fellow Sidney? All the courtiers were scandalised that she should speak in such a heartless fashion, but I understood her meaning perfectly," said Penelope, who had once loved Philip Sidney nearly as much as she now loved Charles.

"This time he will have the Queen's permission," Robin reminded her. "Don't fret, Penelope. He will be far safer at sea."

"Tossing about in the Atlantic, in a little wooden box, infested with rats and fever? Do you call that safe?"

"But Charles has been to sea before. He commanded his own ship in the battle against the Armada, which is more than most of us can claim. All I did was to sit on my horse at Tilbury, waiting for an army that never landed."

"Yes, but the Armada fight wasn't like a long sea voyage. I'm not thinking of the danger from the enemy, I'm thinking of his health," she persisted, ignoring Charles's obvious annoyance. "He catches cold very easily. He needs a great deal of sleep . . . "

"Well, my dear, if I take him away from you, perhaps he'll get some," retorted Robin.

Penelope lost her temper. "Be damned to you, Essex!" she blazed at him. "I didn't come here to be a target for your lewdness. I won't stand it!"

"Why, here's a molehill turned into a mountain," said Robin, comically disconcerted. "Was it such a deadly insult? I meant no harm." He glanced from one of his companions to the other.

"Have you taken umbrage too, my lord? I hope you don't mean to challenge me to another duel."

Charles and Robin had actually fought a duel ten years ago. Oddly enough, their friendship dated from that day.

Now Charles was merely amused.

"No need to fly out at Robert," he told Penelope. "You invited that answer, he couldn't resist it."

"You're as bad as he is." Penelope was in a royal rage. "How you stick together, rollicking over your filthy alehouse jests!" She pushed past them, her farthingale swinging with indignation, and marched off down a narrow path into the wood.

She came to anchor in a wilderness of hazel saplings, inwardly seething. Men were all the same, coarse-grained and bawdy. It was outrageous of Robin to take her up like that, and of Charles to encourage him. She had simply been trying to explain that he was not as tough as he pretended; how could she help it if the masculine mind always ran in one direction? The truth was, Robin had hit a random blow at something which might partly account for her wish to keep Charles at home. Was it because she loved him so much that she could not bear to let him go? It was not a very heroic reason. I wouldn't mind, she assured herself, if fighting was his true vocation.

There was a crackle of branches behind her. Charles had come to make peace.

"Robert sends you his apologies; not an easy thing for him, as you know. He didn't mean to offend you."

"Then what did he mean?" snapped Penelope. "He as good as told me that I am — insatiable."

"My darling, he did no such thing. An idle word, flashed back on the spur of the moment! Angel, what's come over you? I've never known you so mealy-mouthed before."

"It's so humiliating. Not Robin's shafts of brotherly wit, I suppose I can put up with those. The plain fact is that you wish to go off and leave me, and you won't listen when I ask you to stay. I'm not accustomed to beg for favours."

"I don't *wish* to leave you! That's the wildest folly, and you know it. Do you suggest that every man in the fleet is running away from his wife? I shall miss you intolerably, and I hope you'll miss me. But men have to fight for their country and their families when the need arises, just as women have to bear children. We can't deny our own natures for fear of getting hurt. Essex wants me with him on this campaign, I feel in honour bound to go, and if you try to prevent me, you are robbing me of my manhood."

Penelope said nothing.

"I shouldn't have to tell you this." Charles spoke with an unusual crispness. "How can you accuse me of wanting to leave you? Do you think I love you any less than I did? Look at me, Penelope. No, don't stand gaping at that tree as though I wasn't here. Look straight at me and tell me if I have given you any cause to doubt me."

She did look at him, inexorably drawn by the strength in his voice and the compelling virility of that dark, level gaze. The pressure he put on her was so intense that it was almost physical. There had never been anything remote or languid about Charles when he was making love. She felt the blood rising under her skin.

"Well," he enquired, "have you any reason to complain, or are you simply indulging yourself by acting a tragedy queen?"

"Acting a tragedy queen," said Penelope, with a meekness that was most unlike her.

"Then let me tell you, my girl, that I find it a most tedious performance."

"So do I," she admitted, capitulating. He could always manage her unruly temper without losing his own.

He took her by the shoulders, gave her a gentle, admonitory shake, and told her he didn't know why he was in love with such a fool. After which they wandered on together through the wood, in a state of restored harmony.

She made no further attempt to stop him joining the expedition.

Everyone they knew seemed to be going. The volunteers included Kit Blount, Rich and Harry Southampton. Robin was in sole command this time, with Lord Thomas Howard as his Vice Admiral, Ralegh as Rear-Admiral and Charles as

Lieutenant-General of the Land Forces.

The fleet sailed in July, but the weather was against them. The English summer was getting worse every year, and the great gale of 1597 tore across the country like an angry tyrant, uprooting trees and flooding rivers. Penelope and Frank, watching the rain shatter against the windows of Essex House, hardly dared to think what it must be like at sea.

The ships limped back into Falmouth by twos and threes. They had taken a fearful buffeting, and many of the soldiers were half-dead with sea-sickness. It was several days before everyone was accounted for; Essex and Ralegh each thought the other had been drowned. One of the invalids was Rich. He did not want to give in, but his brother-in-law was obliged to order him ashore. He had been so ill that another day at sea might have killed him.

Poor Rich came back ignominiously, to be nursed by Penelope. She was extremely sorry for him. She took him down to Leez Priory, their estate in North Essex, and made every effort to be kind, which was not at all easy, because Rich had a genuine reason for being cross, and he made the most of it. It must have added to his annoyance that Charles had come through the ordeal with flying colours, in spite of Penelope's gloomy prophecies about his health. He had never missed a meal.

On the 17th August the Fleet sailed again, and the country waited hopefully for news of another Cadiz.

The news, when it came, was not what they expected. The Islands Voyage could only be described as a failure.

Another storm, and the disabling of some of their best ships, prevented any landings on the Spanish mainland, but it was when they went on to the Azores that the real trouble started. All the original plans went wrong. Ralegh had already vanished once from the Fleet — trying a bit of piracy on his own, said the cynics. Now he did the same thing again. He failed to turn up at an arranged meeting-place, and while Essex was cruising around looking for him, Ralegh blazed into Fayal, landed without his General's permission, and attacked the port. Essex, when at last he got there, was furious. He accused Ralegh of giving him the slip on purpose, in order to make a private bid for military glory. Ralegh retorted that the Lord General's plans had been vague and contradictory — and anyway his lordship had seen fit to change them several times without condescending to tell his Rear-Admiral what they were supposed to be doing. This unedifying scene took place on board *Due Repulse*, in Essex's cabin, with his more excitable supporters spurring him on, saying that Ralegh's actions justified a court-martial.

Tom Howard, the Vice-Admiral, managed to pacify the two very angry commanders, but it was mortifying to find that while they had been quarrelling in the harbour, the Spanish troops had marched out of the Fort and got clean away.

After that, the various skirmishing raids were frustrating and unproductive, and to cap everything, they again missed the loaded Spanish treasure fleet on its annual journey across the Atlantic. The Council of War, now thoroughly sobered, had a hard job concocting a report which would put the best gloss on their performance.

"The fates were against us," declared

Kit Blount, straddling the hearth in the gallery at Essex House, a few days after they got home. "The one thing we might have got out of it was hanging that fox Raleigh. A pity Essex is so chivalrous. He had a legitimate chance of sending the slippery devil where he belongs. We'd all have stood by him."

"Then I hope you would also have gone with him to tell the Queen you'd hanged the Captain of her Guard," remarked Kit's cousin.

Penelope glanced from one to the other. As far as the Blounts were concerned, she had certainly got a better bargain than her mother. Though Kit was a fine-looking man in his way, and three months' active service had tautened up his muscles and reduced his weight. There was still a kind of military swagger about his dress and manner; Sir Gelly Meyrick had it too — Robin's Welsh steward preferred soldiering to stewardship. Harry Southampton was a younger version of the warrior at ease, and Penelope was glad to see that someone, presumably Robin, had made him get his hair cut. In contrast to these martial figures, Charles had reverted to his extreme air of worldly elegance as soon as he got to London and had a bath. He said austerely that a nobleman's mansion was no place for stamping about in your boots and rattling your sword, and he had no use for swashbucklers.

"Hanging Ralegh," mused Southampton, "might have been too dangerous. But we could have brought him back under guard to stand his trial here. He was totally insubordinate."

"I'd advise your lordship to stop brooding over past wrongs," said Charles. "May I remind you all that Essex and Ralegh are now reconciled. There's no sense in stirring up mud among our brother-officers when we have so many fireside warriors shooting at our reputations."

"I wish I understood the campaign better," Penelope said to Charles later. "I find all those Islands so confusing; I can never remember where Fayal is, or Tercera. Will you show me on the map?"

"I've better things to do with you, my darling, than look at maps."

This was all very charming, but as a rule

Charles enjoyed telling her everything that happened to him: he was being curiously evasive about the Islands Voyage.

"I wish you would explain," she persisted. "According to Kit . . . "

"Kit's a blockhead, like most of my family, I regret to say. A melancholy thought assails me: do you think Mount will take after them?"

She was indignant. "How can you speak so of your own son? Mount's half a Devereux, don't forget. He may make a great soldier, like his uncle."

For no one could doubt Essex's essential greatness, and the people adored him as much as ever. War at sea was a hit-or-miss affair; all commanders had an occasional reverse. Even the incomparable Frankie Drake had met with one or two.

The Queen, to be sure, was disagreeable — but then she was critical even of success, and particularly critical, for some obscure reason, of her beloved Essex the moment he went near a warship or a battlefield. Possibly it was the price he paid for her affection; letting him go into danger was an appalling strain on her nerves.

Now she had him safe at home, living at a faster pace than ever, working twice as hard, careering his horses about the tiltyard to get exercise in the few hours he could spare, but there was a curious malaise behind all this activity that Penelope found disturbing. There was something wrong with Robin. It might be his health; the men who served under him said that the General must have a body of iron, but in fact it was his will that was made of iron, and he suffered from violent headaches brought on by exhaustion. Or very likely his conscience was tormenting him, for he had gone back to his former mistress, Elizabeth Bridges, one of the maids of honour. To an onlooker, this infatuation seemed to give him a hectic and entirely sensual form of excitement, it certainly did not bring him peace. And Frank's heartbroken distress would pierce a conscience far less sensitive than Robin's; besides which he had a very stern domestic chaplain who was not afraid of rebuking his patron in the harshest terms. Between his wife and his chaplain, he could not be having much peace at home either. Yet the puzzle remained — how had Robin got himself to such a pass after the high serenity of a year ago? He was quite different since coming home from the Islands.

Penelope mulled all this over, one evening in her little house at Bart's, thinking aloud in a monologue, while Charles went through the lengthy drill of filling and lighting his pipe. He was a heavy smoker, so it was lucky she liked the aromatic scent of tobacco.

"Charles."

"Angel?"

"Was there any trouble in the Azores that I haven't been told of? I have a feeling that you've kept some secret from me."

Charles had got his pipe going at last. She saw him through a haze of smoke. He hesitated, and when he answered, she thought he had changed his mind about what he was going to say.

"Nothing happened in the Islands that you haven't heard twenty times over. You can pass your own judgment."

Part Two

'A Sin to Covet Honour'

April 1598 – June 1599

1

THE courtiers had begun to say that Essex and the Queen were always quarrelling — speaking as though these bouts had darkened the whole of their eleven-year-old relationship, with only a few sunny interludes. Which, as Penelope knew, was nonsense; there had been far more brightness than shadow. In any case, the black patches seemed only to precede an intensified brilliance.

It was easy to think so on St. George's Day, 1598, waiting among the hushed ranks of courtiers in the Presence Chamber for the annual Garter Procession. This was the most formal of state occasions, so she was beside Rich with the other peers and peeresses, the lesser fry ranged behind them. Robin appeared in the doorway of the Privy Gallery, discussing some point of etiquette with the Lord Chamberlain; he wore his scarlet cassock, with his robes slung carelessly over his arm. The spectators were so tightly packed together that the general quickening of interest was a physical sensation.

"There's the Earl Marshal."

The Earl Marshal. It was still a pleasure to hear his new title; he had come by it in a curious way. Last autumn the Queen had suddenly elevated their cousin, Lord Howard of Effingham, to an earldom. Since he was already the Lord Admiral, this gave him precedence over all the existing earls. Robin was furious. He had no personal grudge against Howard, but he deduced, quite correctly, that the Queen was using this left-handed means to punish her other principal commander for his recent failure in the Islands. It was a public humiliation, and he would not stand it. He took himself off to Wanstead, refusing to come to Court unless the new Lord Nottingham's patent was withdrawn.

His more cautious friends, like Francis Bacon, were horrified. They said he was mad to challenge the Queen, especially on such an issue because, however much she wanted her favourite back, she could hardly withdraw Nottingham's earldom; Essex would have to climb down, and then he would look a fool. They were wrong. After six weeks of hankering for her darling, it was the Queen's will that broke. She did not degrade Nottingham, but she did something for Essex that was even more satisfactory, by reviving an office which was in abeyance. She made him Earl Marshal of England. It was the most glorious prize she had to bestow, giving him a perpetual precedence over Nottingham and everyone else except the Archbishops. He was now, in status as in fact, the greatest man in the kingdom.

So much for Francis Bacon and all the Jeremiahs, thought Penelope, noting the look of well-being that Robin always had when he was happy. There were various whispered comments, and in this silent company they travelled further than the speakers intended.

"You can't deny there's something royal about him. A drop of Plantagenet blood goes a long way."

"God grant it doesn't go too far."

Several more Knights appeared in the doorway. Penelope picked out one in particular. Again there was an outbreak of whispering.

"We never thought to see Mountjoy in these trappings. Ah well, I suppose great lords have their own version of the Ten Commandments. Great ladies too."

Penelope felt Rich stiffen. Their immediate neighbours began to talk rather loudly. She fanned herself with an air of lazy unconcern. She had learnt to ignore such darts of spite, and nothing was going to interfere with her pleasure in seeing Charles as a new Knight of the Garter. She had always been afraid that he might be excluded from this most precious and sacred honour because of the scandal in their private life. But the Queen, when she chose, could be remarkably kind — and perhaps she understood how much that honour meant to a man who had not dared to hope for it. Penelope was grateful to her.

The group in the doorway vanished, and there was an expectant pause. Distant music, as the clergy and choir approached, leading the way towards the chapel. Various Court dignitaries came next, and then the climax: the Garter Procession. The Sovereign of the Order, moving majestically beneath the great canopy which six of the Knights held high above her head. They wore robes of purple velvet, trailing on the ground and lined with white taffetas, scarlet hoods thrown back over the shoulder and small feathered caps. As the Queen passed, her subjects knelt, sweeping down like a field of corn before a strong wind. Penelope's attention was fixed on the two Knights who carried the front poles of the canopy. Sir Robert Devereux and Sir Charles Blount — there was not much to choose between them for looks; they surpassed all the others and Penelope thought that Charles surpassed Robin. He was the more graceful, and the heraldic splendour was perfectly set off by his dark colouring. She might be prejudiced; after six years she was still so much in love that all her pictures of him were touched with emotion. Though today he seemed almost a stranger. His face, like Robin's face, and the Queen's, was gravely intent, as though they were all absorbed by some inward vision. They had relinquished their positive, individual characters to become the representatives of that undying conception of chivalry which stretched across the centuries from

Edward III and the Black Prince.

Spring passed into summer and the surface of life at Court was as smooth as a millpond. No one wanted to cross the Earl Marshal these days. Robert Cecil was friendly and obliging, and Robin had never fallen out with his Howard cousins, in spite of the contest over Nottingham's title.

"Which is just as well," remarked Penelope to Nottingham's daughter Elizabeth Southwell, one afternoon in July when they were sitting in the Privy Gallery. "You and I can't afford to fight, Eliza. We know too many of each other's secrets."

"I never fight with anyone except my husband," protested Lady Elizabeth, a beautiful featherhead. She yawned, glancing towards the carved oak doorway where Anthony Killigrew, the Groom of the Privy Chamber, stood erect and solitary at his post. "What a tedious time they take over their deliberations. Who's in there with her, do you know? Apart from your brother and my father?"

"Only Cecil, I think, and the clerk.

They are choosing a new Lord Deputy for Ireland."

At that moment there was a sound of angry voices inside the Privy Chamber. Every ear in the Gallery was pricked. The Queen, of course, but even more alarming, a man's voice over-riding hers. Suddenly the door flew open, and Mr. Killigrew was nearly knocked over as Nottingham propelled Robin firmly out of the room. Robin was struggling with him.

"I'll not bear such an insult," he shouted. "I wouldn't have stood it from King Harry the Eighth himself, and I'll not stand it from a King in petticoats!"

He broke away from Nottingham and turned, and they saw his face, white and rigid with fury. He strode down the Gallery to the far end, pushed the guard out of his way, and slammed out. No one had the resolution to stop him.

Nottingham had withdrawn into the Privy Chamber, now ominously silent.

In the stunned interval that followed, Penelope stood up. Her only thought was that she must get to Robin.

Charles, who had been talking to Fulke Greville, stopped her with a small gesture.

"I'll go after him, Lady Rich. It's better so."

"If you will, my lord."

She stayed where she was. The gabble of comment that broke out all round her might have been in a foreign language. Then Lord Nottingham emerged once more and came straight across to her. He took her elbow and drew her into one of the oriel windows.

"My lord, what happened?"

"He tried to draw his sword on the Queen."

"Tried to draw — I can't believe it!"

"I assure you, it's true. I think he was out of his mind; in such frenzies he's hardly sane."

"But what was the cause?"

"There was a disagreement over the Irish appointment. Essex spoke very insolently to Her Majesty and turned his back on her, whereupon she boxed his ears and told him to go and be hanged. Well, I own it was beneath her dignity, yet it's not for us to judge her, and in any case, for Essex to act and speak as he did — you heard him — was not far short of treason."

Penelope stared at the Lord Admiral. He was a fine-looking man, with his white hair and very blue eyes, she had known him all her life. And now he was practically accusing Robin of treason. Robin, of all people.

"Cousin Charles," slipping back into the old name from her childhood, "what will she do?"

"She has not yet said. She is very angry: however, her affection for him is so strong — if you can have him back in the Privy Chamber, on his knees and duly penitent, within the hour, I think she might be merciful. But he must be prepared to humble himself as never before, and to accept whatever punishment she chooses to inflict. Will you go and tell him that? He'll listen to you sooner than any of us."

"I'll try to persuade him. Lord Mountjoy is with him now."

But Charles was coming back up the Gallery, threading his way imperviously through the curious courtiers.

"What did he say?" she asked, as Charles reached them.

"He said he'd suffered a deadly injury;

he's taken a horse and ridden off to Wanstead. Why did she hit him?"

Nottingham ignored the question. "Didn't you try to stop him?"

"No, my lord. When two such fierce spirits are at war, it's safer they should put some miles between them. The distance may prevent any further explosions."

"Yes," said Howard thoughtfully. "There's good sense in that. I wish Essex had a little of your moderation, Mountjoy. As it is," turning to Penelope, "I think you will have to go to Wanstead after your brother, my dear. You aren't in attendance on Her Majesty? Then I can make your excuses here."

Before she had time to answer, Charles asked again, "Would your lordship kindly tell me why she hit him? Essex didn't seem to know."

Howard snorted. "Essex knew well enough." He described the incident once more.

"I guessed it was something of the sort, though he utterly denies any provocation. Madam, I think Lord Nottingham is right; you should certainly go to Wanstead."

So instead of dancing away the evening

in galliards and corantos, as she had expected, Penelope found herself travelling down by coach to Robin's country house.

Not that she was able to accomplish anything when she got there. Robin was still in a tearing rage. He was glad to have Penelope with him, but only as an audience. He would not tolerate such treatment, he stormed; no man who struck him would live an hour afterwards, and the humiliation of a blow from a woman seemed to have a perverse horror for him. He, the lineal descendant of the Seigneurs of Evreux, was not to be degraded by the grand-daughter of a Welsh squire. Pride of sex and pride of race had possessed him like two demons.

Frank was at Wanstead already, with her two children and several of Penelope's, Riches and Blounts. The children were banished to the furthest corners of the house and garden, while Robin's wife and sister tried unsuccessfully to console him.

Inevitably, the frantic and exhausting tension took its toll: Robin began his usual grinding headaches and went to bed, saying he was very ill. It would be a blessed release if he died, no one wanted him. Frank nursed him devotedly; his elder sister was so irritated by this mood of self-pity that she would gladly have boxed his ears herself.

All the time their nerves were on wires; they were waiting for the clatter of armed horsemen in the avenue, with a warrant to arrest the man who had so far forgotten his allegiance that he had tried to draw his sword on his Sovereign. No soldiers came, only friends with encouraging news. If the Earl would come back to the Palace in a proper state of contrition, they were sure the Queen would forgive him. There would be no retribution.

This was an amazing proof of his power over her, but it was not what Robin wanted. Recovered from his headaches, he was now calm but deeply ill-used. He absolutely denied that he had done anything to justify the Queen's monstrous behaviour. He had not been insolent, he had not touched his sword, he had simply been the victim of irrational tyranny. Far from apologising to the Queen, he thought the boot should be on the other foot.

Everyone with the slightest influence at Court tried to reason with him, but they could not reach him through the barrier of his own preconceptions. He was innocent, he would not plead guilty, for all the bribes she could offer him. Penelope believed he was sincere. She suspected that Robin's occasional outbursts of violence had the effect of making him drunk; he really did not remember what he had done or said.

The whole country was disturbed by this rift between the Queen and her most exalted subject, and the people were all on his side. At Court it was otherwise, his recent display of obstinacy, over Lord Nottingham's title, had earned him a good many critics, who scoffed at the common herd for being so infatuated with the handsome Earl Marshal that they could see no faults in him. Here they were unjust. The people judged Essex by their own experience of him: the devout, sweet-tempered and modest gentleman who moved among them with such friendly courtesy could never have behaved so atrociously to the Queen. His good manners were proverbial, and as for pride, he showed less sign of it than any nobleman in the kingdom. The story was obviously a slander (probably invented by crooked little Cecil or the hated Ralegh) and they rejected it.

Penelope had seen both aspects of her brother, and was fully aware of the contradictions.

"I can't make you out," she said to him one day. They were sitting on a grassy bank in the garden. "Why does the Queen arouse these passions in you that the rest of us never see? You are the most loving husband and father, the kindest son and brother, an unchanging friend. The Spaniards commend your chivalry as a conqueror. You know, better than most great lords, how to be patient with your servants and dependents, and they all worship you. Why are you so different with her? And don't tell me again how she boxed your ears, for I'm sick of hearing it, and it's not the whole story: you've been flying into tantrums over Her Majesty ever since you were nineteen. Why?"

"You must indeed think you are safe, if you dare to say so much." There was a faint quiver of amusement, and the curtain of melancholy lifted slightly. Even in his depths of sullen gloom there was a haunting quality about him, implicit in the finely set bones and those wonderful eyes. It was the face of a poet, a visionary.

"The Queen? She can bring out the worst in all of us, when it suits her egotism. Better break step with the music than dance to her tune, like the rest of the fools."

He was plucking the petals off a daisy, savagely, like a boy mutilating an insect. Penelope found herself asking the question that nagged at the back of her mind.

"Robin. How much does the Queen — do you still retain your affection for her?"

He gave her a look of desolation.

"Affection? Is that what you call it? The blind idolatry of a young troubadour with a head full of dreams? How green I was! She's killed all that, with this cursed life she makes me lead. I wish to God we had a man on the Throne!"

Though he had spoken very quietly, they both glanced round in case anyone was near enough to hear that dangerous admission. They were quite alone, apart from two small figures, spinning like tops, at the far end of the bowling alley: Robert Hereford and his cousin Harry Rich, competing to see who could turn the most cartwheels.

"If that's treason," said Robin, "she's driven me to it. How would you like to endure my fate, year after year? The endless hypocrisy, the dishing-up of stale compliments, the patting and pawing from those old hands? Oh, nothing more indecorous, I assure you; I doubt if she's ever gone much further. Heaven knows how Leicester stood it when they were both twenty-five. Who but an old maid could relish such paltry toying? And as for her goading me into these rages, that's deliberate; haven't you yet understood why she does it? She does it, my sweet Penelope, for the pleasure of being frightened a little, and then submitting to my will over some trifle — so that she can enjoy a mimicry of that surrender she would never make to a lover in the days when she had the chance." He saw his sister's expression of incredulous distaste. "No, you would never think of that. Anyone who's seen you with Charles can guess how your surrenders are made: you are honest and fearless, you rejoice in the purpose for which you were created. The women I've loved have all been of your stamp. I've never had any truck with sterile dalliance, but in this one instance. My Queen has made us both contemptible."

He was leaning with one elbow on the grass; he turned, pillowing his head in his arms. There was something defeated in the way he lay there, so still, his body pressed against the turf. Penelope was appalled. This explained why he had become so impossible in his dealings with the Queen. And yet — was it the whole truth? He had shown her some of the letters he had sent to the Palace during his self-imposed exile. She remembered one sentence: *When I think how I have preferred your beauty above all things, and received no pleasure in life but by the increase of your favour towards me, I wonder at myself what cause there could be to make me absent myself one day from you* ... Could that be completely false? Certainly, if a man like Ralegh had written it. But Robin was a bad liar, a bad actor. She thought that this aversion to a most unnatural relationship was only one broken link in the strong invisible chain that bound him to Elizabeth.

"Dear Robin," she said, "I am so truly sorry. I had no idea how hard it was for you to bear."

She did not know how to go on, for she did not see how he could escape from his odious position as the old woman's darling without wrecking the career which had become the mainspring of his existence. It struck her that the Queen and Robin had reversed their original aims. At nineteen, Robin had little idea of policy and no ambition; it was the Queen herself who had fascinated him, and his early lessons had been learnt merely to please her. It was she who had wanted to make him into a statesman, until she discovered that, instead of an obedient house-dog, she had been nourishing a young lion — an active Protestant warrior whose sense of their country's destiny differed widely from her own time-serving caution. She would gladly push him out of public affairs, thought Penelope, were it not for the dread of losing her favourite. And he would just as gladly give up the role of favourite, but for his equal dread of losing his Prince's good will, which was essential to a general and a statesman. For the past two or three years, each had been paying unwillingly for what the other did not want to give; no wonder they were so bitterly unsatisfied. But there did not seem to be any possible solution as long as the Queen lived.

Without stirring, Robin told her to go away and leave him in peace. She hesitated, yet she saw he needed privacy more than the useless pity which was all she had to offer. Feeling inadequate, and miserable, she went, her wide skirt brushing lightly over the grass.

The Council was frantic over Robin's absence, because it was growing increasingly difficult to govern the country without him. Apart from his various official duties, he was the controller of his own foreign intelligence service, on which the nation had come to depend. Anthony Bacon was receiving five times as many letters and reports from abroad as his cousin Robert Cecil received on behalf of the Government. It was a fantastic situation, due to the Queen's cheeseparing economy; she had profited by Essex's enterprise, allowing him to turn himself into a Foreign Secretary of State, if such a post could be imagined, entirely in his private capacity, and now he had cut off the supply of information. Their lordships kept insisting that Essex must be got back at all costs.

He was longing to return — as a Councillor. In August old Lord Burleigh died. This would mean many changes in the administration. Essex walked in the procession at Burleigh's funeral, but he could not resume his public life until he had made his peace with the Queen, and he still refused the apology she demanded.

Two months after the quarrel he went down with a severe attack of his recurrent ague. For the Queen, this was the final straw: she wanted the Earl Marshal back at work as much as any of her

Council, she wanted the man far more. The thought of his broken health swept away the last remnants of her anger. She sent him a message that he might come to Court when he chose. He need make no admission of guilt, no reference to the past, the whole episode would be ignored.

His illness was perfectly genuine, but the cause was more nervous than physical, and this was the cure for it. Five days later he was well enough to go to the Palace.

Matters were made very smooth for him; he slipped in one evening by a side entrance. The Queen was in the Privy Chamber with only two attendants: Penelope and Lady Scrope, one of their Carey cousins who was particularly attached to Robin. There were no unfriendly witnesses when Mr. Killigrew announced the Earl of Essex.

He came in slowly, and knelt with a stiff formality, a long way from the Queen's chair.

"I am glad to see you, my lord. I trust you are recovered." The Queen was ill at ease; she did not know how he was going to behave, and that must be why she had not met him alone. Penelope had only recently suspected that the Queen was afraid of Robin, and if she had originally encouraged that sensation, there was no longer any pleasure in it.

"I thank Your Majesty, I am quite restored." His tone was arctic.

"These agues have ever been a trial to you."

"Not so great a trial as Your Majesty's unmerited cruelty . . . "

"Don't start on that," she broke in urgently. Then her manner changed. "Essex, come here."

The voice was vibrant, compelling, and as she sat erect and slender in the dusk, the light just gleaming on her pearls, she managed somehow to create the illusion of a strange and timeless beauty that kept its own perfection.

Robin reacted to that mysterious appeal; he went to her at once and knelt again, kissing the delicate fingers that were extended to him, his head bowed. With her other hand, the Queen stroked his hair. Penelope, remembering what he had said about patting and pawing, watched in acute discomfort. And then she saw a marvellous transformation. The Queen's hand ran along the line of the temple where she had struck him, all those weeks ago; she might have been healing a wound, for as this reconciling touch conveyed its message, he looked up, his eyes shone with their old brilliance, and he gave her his sudden, charming smile.

She was smiling too. After a pause she said: "You are very silent, can I have put a spell on you? As a rule you have plenty to say, even when it isn't what I choose to hear."

"Madam, you know that I am overcome by the joy of being reunited with Your Majesty."

It was too convincing to be taken for flattery.

"Well, I have many things to say to you. No, you shall not kneel any longer; you must guard your strength." Adroitly, the Queen lightened the atmosphere; she did not speak of the political problems they would have to face in the morning, nor of her sorrow at the loss of Burleigh, but talked cheerfully of small concerns. "I had a gift from an old scholar last week that I have been saving to share with you, knowing that your appetite for history is as devouring as mine. Lady Rich, where is the book that I wished to show to the Earl Marshal?"

Penelope fetched it, and he took it from her and brought the candles closer, moving with an alert confidence. Soon he and the Queen were poring over the book, reading bits aloud to each other and wandering off into the byways of antiquity. Presently Penelope and Lady Scrope were dismissed. They retired, leaving those two alone together, as they had so often been before, in the intimacy which Robin said he hated. He looked remarkably content.

During the next few days, while he was getting back into the swim, Penelope did not see much of him. At the end of the week he came to her lodging in the Palace, and prowled about in a restless and inconsequent way, fidgeting with her ornaments. It was obvious that he had something to say and could not get it out. At last she was obliged to help him.

"I'm delighted to receive you, but it grows late, and I have to change my dress for the masque. Robin, do put that Venetian goblet down before you break it, and tell me what you want."

"It's no great matter. At least — Penelope, there was a time at Wanstead, when I was in the darkest pit of despair, that I said some things I wish you had not heard. I should like you to blot out that afternoon as though it had never happened."

"Agreed," she said. "Any confidence of yours is safe with me; I'd never repeat it, even to Charles. Surely you knew that already?"

"Good grief, I'm not doubting your discretion. I didn't ask you to keep your mouth shut, I asked you to forget. My conscience assails me when I recall the picture I drew of Her Majesty. It was false, unchivalrous and — and altogether dastardly. I must have been mad." He flushed, staring at the ground. "She has been so very good to me, and I do love her most dearly. When I am with her, and she is kind, she brings a meaning to my life that I should never have found without her. She has always been my guiding star and inspiration."

Yes, there were many confused and contradictory elements in his feeling for the Queen. His resentment might have taught him to assess one side of her character only too clearly; he was unable to fathom his own.

2

DURING the weeks that followed, the appointment of a Lord Deputy for Ireland became more and more urgent, and the Council was still undecided. Essex was again being difficult. Back in favour, he was convinced that he had found out how to manage the Queen for her own good. He had won two major victories over her in the last year by a technique of rigid obstinacy, and he soon saw that she was not going to risk a third engagement. The discussions were further complicated because no one could discover what the Earl Marshal really thought about the Irish problem. He simply attacked every suggestion made by anyone else.

At one point Mountjoy was considered as a possible candidate, but Essex opposed his nomination.

"Whereupon I am told their lordships dropped the notion like a hot brick," said Charles. "They are a great deal more frightened of Essex than they are of Tyrone and all his rebels." He was standing in front of the fire in Penelope's withdrawing-room; she was back in her own house again, and expecting another baby in the spring. She heard him with mixed feelings, relief predominating. The idea of Charles going to Ireland horrified her. Her father had died of dysentery in that fatal country which destroyed men's health, wrecked their reputations and broke their hearts. All the same she was sorry for Charles who seemed quite unreasonably upset.

"Of course Robin would not let them send you — I never heard anything so outrageous. He needs you too much here."

"I wish I could flatter myself with such a myth. Would you care to know your brother's true opinion of me? It was reported to me verbatim. He told the Council that I am utterly unfit for the post of Lord Deputy; my estate is mean, my followers few, besides which I have small experience in the wars, and I am too bookish to make a general."

"Oh," said Penelope, taken aback.

"It's very salutary," commented Charles, "to know how my dearest friend rates my value to the State."

"But Charles — he can't have meant it. Not in that precise fashion. And it's true you have no experience as commander-in-chief."

"Nor ever shall have, after being damned with such an epithet. Too bookish! I could have borne the rest, but that's a stab in the back, coming from Essex. Since when has he decided that soldiers ought to be illiterate?"

Charles moved abruptly, knocking over a stool. It was most unusual for him to be clumsy. Today, for the first time, he made the house in Bart's Priory seem small, far too small for a nobleman in a very bad temper. "It's as plain as a pikestaff what Essex is after. He wants to go to Ireland himself."

"Surely not? You know he always insists that directly he leaves the Court, Cecil and Ralegh manage to turn the Queen against him. Why should he wish to go to Ireland, of all places?"

"To prove to us all how splendidly he can play Alexander. Or to prove it to himself, to allay his own doubts. Heaven help him if he does go. He'll make even more mistakes than he did in the Islands — if that were possible."

"What do you mean?" she demanded.

"I mean," said Charles, "that Essex is a very incompetent general."

She stared at him, dumbfounded. "How can you say that? He's the best general we have, everyone admits it. He's fought in more campaigns than any of them ... "

"Yes, five. And what do they show? In the Low Countries he was a boy, he had no say in the conduct of the war, nor in Portugal either. In France he was subordinate to King Henry. Cadiz ... "

"Well, what of Cadiz?" she challenged him. "You can't call that the work of an incompetent general. His triumph at Cadiz was praised all over Europe."

"Granted, Cadiz was an epic. But it was no masterpiece of strategy, no such refinements were needed there. Once the Port had fallen, they had to take the City; the greenest recruit could have seen so far. What followed was the action of a most valiant and resolute captain, magnified by the numbers involved and the glory of the prize. Essex is the bravest man I know, and a burning inspiration of courage in others. He is not a general. He can no more plan a campaign than I can spin yarn. When it came to the Islands — you've often asked what went wrong out there: well, I'll tell you. The Lord General failed to produce any clear design, and the whole expedition was a shambles. He flew from one purpose to another, changing his orders half a dozen times as he went; he was like a child who has learnt the moves on a chessboard without any understanding of the game. And this is the man who presumes to tell the Council that I am not fit to cross swords with Tyrone."

It was all such complete heresy to Penelope that it did not penetrate beyond the surface of her mind. She was more disturbed because Charles, of all people, was giving this extraordinary exhibition of pique and resentment.

"I did not think you could be so disloyal," she said coldly.

"Is that what you call it? When I've kept my mouth shut ever since, because my judgment and my affection were on different sides?" He paused and looked at her; there was something helpless and baffled in his expression. "This is Greek to you, isn't it, Penelope?"

"On the contrary, I can easily construe it. Essex has wounded your pride, so you are hunting round for any accusation you can hurl against him. It seems a paltry kind of revenge for a man of your lordship's breeding."

Charles flushed. "If that's what you think, I'd better go. It's a waste of time trying to tell the truth to a Devereux."

He took himself off in a most unusual fit of sulks, and she immediately began to feel guilty, as though she had somehow failed him. Poor Charles, he must have been very unhappy; only a really bitter sense of humiliation could have goaded him into talking such ill-tempered nonsense. She forgot her championship of Robin — who needed no champions anyway — in her concern for Charles.

She did not waste time wondering whether he wanted the Irish appointment; she could think of nothing less likely to attract him. It was one thing to go off with a host of friends and to fight for the Protestant cause at sea or on the Continent; the lonely and disheartening business of trying to govern Ireland was a different matter entirely. A procession of hardened generals had gone there and failed, each finding that his reputation at home had suffered as a consequence. Charles would certainly appreciate the dangers there. No, he could not want to go; it must be the fact that Essex had ruined his chances, and in such a mortifying way, which he minded so much. That was something she could attempt to put right.

She went to Court that evening, shimmering in silver satin and crystals. At three months, the baby had not begun to show, and she could still afford the most exotic fashions. She cornered Robin in the Presence Chamber after supper; he was looking particularly carefree and invincible.

"And what can I do for you, Pen?" he asked amiably.

"You can allow me to pick a bone with you. How did you come to shatter Charles's pretensions so brutally before the Council? Surely there was no need to be so outspoken? You've hurt him desperately, Robin."

He was startled, and then indignant. Charles had no business to know what was said in Council. Their discussions were highly confidential.

"What's that to the point?" she retorted. "He does know, and I should have thought, after all these years, that you might have bargained for that. Haven't you realised that if you speak slightingly of one of your own party, Cecil will see to it that someone babbles? He'd love to drive a wedge between you and Charles." And he might well succeed. She thought of Charles's disparaging remarks, which she was certainly not going to repeat. "You've wounded his feelings and his pride; I've never known him so put out, quite unlike himself."

"I suppose I should have guessed what would happen," said Robin slowly. He was obviously distressed. He never gossiped himself, and was frequently astonished by other people's calculated spite. "As though I should ever wish to cause him pain! What a viper he must think me. But indeed, he isn't the man for Ireland,

and I can't believe you wanted us to send him there."

"Of course I didn't. Though I can't see why you had to stress his lack of ability. Charles is no carpet knight, as you've reminded me yourself before now."

"Good God, I never impugned his valour. He's the bravest man alive. It's not his fault that he wasn't cut out to be a general."

He was using almost the same terms that Charles had used of him, it was very odd.

"When he served under you in the Islands," she asked, "did you have any difference of opinion?"

Robin played with the links of his gold chain, frowning slightly. "He was a little too eager to talk out of turn; he seemed to forget that I was his commanding officer, and not simply your brother. I was obliged to give him a formal reprimand. It was a most uncomfortable occasion for us both."

So that was it. Poor Charles. She did not want to hear any more, it seemed like spying on him. She gazed across

113

the Presence Chamber; the dazzle of lights, striking sparks of reflection from so many jewels, confused the vision, yet it was easy to find Charles. He had kept away from her all the evening; he was standing behind one of the card tables, talking idly to a couple of friends. Among the other gesticulating courtiers, bright as parrots in their blue and saffron, emerald and carmine, Lord Mountjoy stood out in his uncompromising black doublet, slashed with white. That, and his gift for keeping still, gave him an immense distinction. She felt a stir of pleasure and admiration, being old enough to preserve these sensations even when she discovered that her darling had been making a fool of himself.

"We ought not to forget," she said, "that Charles is more vulnerable than most of our kind. He comes of the old nobility, as we do, but his family were so impoverished, he has had such a hard struggle. The boy who wasn't thought good enough to be my husband — who would have dreamed that he might one day be suggested as Lord Deputy of Ireland, the Queen's viceroy? Even the honour of being considered is an achievement."

"And I've spoilt it for him," said Robin remorsefully. "With my over-zealous tongue. Well, that shall be put right, the sooner the better. I must make my peace with him."

He stood up. Penelope had an instinct to restrain him, but it was too late. He was heading across the wide floor towards Charles, an almost royal progress, as everyone stood aside to let him pass. She could only hope that Charles would be conciliating. Their meeting did not encourage her. At a range of fifty feet she could see him being so extremely deferential to the Earl Marshal that his respect bordered on insolence. Her heart sank.

At this moment the French Ambassador approached her, blocking her view. There was a delicate matter he was anxious to discuss, he needed her assistance.

"I should be delighted to help your excellency," murmured Penelope, wishing he would sit down.

He chose to remain planted in front of her. By moving a little, she got a glimpse of Robin, talking fast and emphatically, while Charles listened with a face of stone. Presently Charles shrugged and turned away. Robin caught his arm, and somehow pushed or persuaded him into the oriel window, out of sight. It was unbearably tantalising. Penelope tried to concentrate on the Ambassador.

His request was following a familiar pattern. Could she ask her brother to ask the Queen — and so forth. She settled, abstractedly, to the role of the favourite's favourite sister.

"I'm sure you can handle this with advantage, madam," the Ambassador concluded at last. "And here, by good fortune, is Monseigneur now."

Penelope blinked and glanced round. And here, indeed, were Robin and Charles, apparently in perfect harmony.

"Monseigneur, I have a suit to make to you, but I shall leave Madame la Baronne to explain it, she is a more accomplished diplomat than I." The Frenchman bowed and moved away.

"Madame la Baronne is a mistress of diplomacy," said Robin when he had gone. "Here is another treaty of your making, Pen. Charles has forgiven me my ill-chosen phrases, as I knew he would. Not through any merit of mine, but because he is too generous to bear a grudge."

How impossible it was to withstand, that absolute confidence. Having been thoughtless and unkind, Robin was sorry, and he had said so. He had trusted Charles to meet him halfway. And of course he had been justified, though Charles now seemed a little confused, avoiding Penelope's eye when Robin spoke of his generosity.

"The truth is," he said, "that I can't quarrel with you, Robert. Other people manage it, but I haven't the knack."

They all laughed, and there the whole matter was shelved. A few minutes later Mr. Killigrew arrived with a summons for Robin from the Queen.

Watching him go, Charles said: "There's a quality of innocence about Robert that puts my devious nature to shame ... Penelope, may I come home with you tonight? Or don't you want me?"

"That's a very foolish question."

"Is it? You were glad enough to see the back of me this morning."

"Because I love you too well to risk a clash between us. If you can't quarrel with Robin, why then, I daren't quarrel with you, my darling. I understand that you were talking wildly in order to relieve your mortification."

Charles did not contradict her.

And when, a few weeks later, Robin was appointed Lord Deputy of Ireland, Charles was the first to offer his congratulations. Though if, as he maintained, Robin had been working for this all along, he now showed a curious lack of enthusiasm.

Most generals might have been expected to feel a certain reluctance about this particular post, but no one imagined that Essex was brooding over the fate of his predecessors. He had a reputation for achieving the impossible, and apart from his ability, and his tremendous prestige, he was being given the finest army that had ever been sent over there; at last there was a real hope of hammering the Irish, and he was going to get the credit. He was probably less concerned over the troubles ahead than over the troubles he was leaving behind.

He had picked up a mysterious rumour

118

that Sir Robert Cecil had been bought by the Spaniards and that when the Queen died he would try to seize the English crown for the Infanta. At a first hearing, this sounded incredible; the Secretary of State was such a zealous hounder of Catholics — more from policy than piety, his true religion being the advancement of the house of Cecil. On the other hand, it must be remembered that he had always wanted to make peace with Spain. He undoubtedly knew by now that Essex meant to support the King of Scots, and if that plan succeeded, he himself would be squeezed out of power; it would serve him better to secure the inheritance for a candidate of his own choosing. Were these reasons strong enough to make him decide that London was worth a Mass?

Robin could not make up his mind about the story. He and Cecil were on very good terms, they played cards together every evening, and exchanged private jokes. But behind his superficial confidence Penelope sensed a faint malaise; he was wondering what manoeuvres the little man would get up to in his absence.

And if this anxiety was hypothetical, there was a more urgent one that couldn't be shelved — before he could start for Ireland he needed to raise a large sum of money. A high military command was always expensive, and as usual he was terribly in debt. He had got to retrench somehow, and the only available method was a drastic one. He would have to sell Wanstead.

This was a blow to the whole family, and especially to Penelope, who loved the beautiful house in the forest as though it was her own. Wanstead had poignant memories of Philip Sidney; she did not want to lose touch with those, and it was there that she had first met Charles. In the last few years they had escaped to her brother's house as often as they could. There was nowhere else they could go for complete privacy and freedom.

"I can't endure it," she told Charles in despair. "To be shut out of our paradise. Nothing will ever be the same again."

"Are we so dependent on bricks and trees?"

Charles was taking it very calmly, though he had spent a lot of time and thought improving Wanstead, because he had a passion for gardening and adorning fine rooms. Robin had always been too busy.

"How can you dismiss the bricks and trees so lightly?" she asked. "To me, they are alive. We've built part of ourselves into that place. Doesn't it enrage you to picture some odious stranger lolling in the galleries, swaggering on the terraces, digging up all your rare plants?"

"It will hardly be a stranger. Someone from the Court, more like."

"That will be worse," she grumbled.

"Are you so certain, Penelope? Is there no one but Essex whom you could accept as the owner of Wanstead?"

"How could there be? I can't expect Rich to buy the place, and there's no one else can give me back my state of privilege. Unless — Charles!" She was arrested by the mixture of triumph and teasing in his manner. "Surely you can't be toying with the notion — it's impossible."

"Why? My estate is not so mean as it has been painted."

"That's evident," she said slowly, "if

you intend to bid for Wanstead."

Charles never talked about money, unlike Rich, who talked of nothing else, or Robin, hounded by his debts. Charles kept his own counsel; both his fortune and his career had grown out of very small beginnings, and he never drew attention to his progress. She had no idea how much he could raise, in cash or credit.

"Can you afford such an outlay?" She wondered with a twinge of guilt, whether her complaining had undermined his good sense. It would be wicked to batten on his devotion. "I can't let you beggar yourself to satisfy my whims."

"There's no risk of that. I need a house near London while I am so constantly employed on the Queen's business; my property in the West Country is too far off. Now I can have the one I desire above all others, besides doing Essex a service. And I hope he will let me return his years of hospitality; I don't think he will dislike coming to his old home if it remains in the family. For that's what it amounts to. I may not hand you the title deeds as a gift; we must pretend that you come there as my guest, and always take a few chosen friends along with us to lend a mantle of discretion. But once you are inside the gates, every inch of the demesne will be yours, all your wishes and commands will be obeyed, you will be the mistress of Wanstead. At last I shall have a proper setting for you, where I can pay you the honour due to my wife."

She recognised that this was something immensely important to him. Had he been striving secretly, for years, towards the time when he could provide a 'proper setting' for her — this self-disciplined and elusive man who never stopped surprising her?

"I had not imagined anything so perfect," she said. "To share Wanstead with you, it surpasses all my dreams. And how to thank you — I'm like the Queen of Sheba, bereft of words." Even the sudden delight of knowing that the house was safe came second to her surge of feeling for Charles: tenderness, gratitude and a most unusual humility. "I don't deserve to be so happy. Dear Charles, you are too generous. It's disgraceful how you spoil me."

"Yes, it is," he agreed. "I can't help it. You're so well worth spoiling, Angel."

Robin was very glad to let Charles buy the estate. He too saw it as a family arrangement; Charles was like a brother to him. Robin wanted to take him to Ireland as his second-in-command, and Charles was prepared to serve under the man who had edged him out of the senior post. He had quite overcome his grievances. But the Queen refused to let him go, which was a relief to Penelope. Robin would have one Blount with him, his young stepfather, and his other great friend, Harry Southampton. Harry had been having troubles of his own. He had fallen in love with Elizabeth Vernon, one of the Maids of Honour, and married her secretly in a great hurry after she became pregnant. When the story got out, the bride and bridegroom had been packed off to prison, where they languished for several months, not quite certain which offence they were being punished for. Marriage, in the Queen's eyes, was probably a worse sin than fornication. They had just been set free, but were still in disgrace, and Harry was hoping for a little military glory to restore him to favour.

The new Lord Deputy left London on the 27th March, 1599. Though she was expecting her baby very soon, Penelope was determined to catch a parting glimpse of her brother. She and Frank, who was also with child, watched and waved as he rode away, both struggling with an anguish of tears and pride.

Robin always looked his best on horseback: his athletic vigour and great height were emphasised by the glittering breastplate, the tall toss of his plumes. He smiled and saluted the cheering crowds, never losing the patrician dignity he could bring to a formal occasion. A huge concourse of citizens lined the streets to wish him Godspeed. At thirty-one he was among the most famous figures in Europe: the Right Honourable Sir Robert Devereux, Earl of Essex and Ewe, Viscount Hereford, Baron Ferrars of Chartley, Bourchier and Lovain, Knight of the Most Noble Order of the Garter, Earl Marshal of England, Lord Lieutenant and Governor-General of Ireland, Member of Her Majesty's Most

Honourable Privy Council, Master of the Ordnance, Master of the Horse, Chancellor of the University of Cambridge. The sum total of inheritance and achievement was tremendous, and no one else could have carried it with such distinction.

After he had gone life contracted to a domestic scale. Penelope's son was born a fortnight later and christened St. John. As soon as she could travel, she went to Wanstead, taking young Lady Southampton with her to lend an air of propriety — not the most likely choice for a duenna perhaps, but the poor girl was moping for Harry and needed a change.

Charles and Penelope were blissfully contented that spring; riding in the beechwoods, spending long mornings conferring with the gardeners. The quiet continuity and the absorbing details gave them an illusion of married life. It was a particular joy for Charles to have his four children under his own roof. The little girls, Penny and Isabel, were so pretty, with their shining eyes and dark curls; he gave them each a pony, and there would be one for Mount directly he was old enough. A lively and exhausting child,

Mount darted everywhere in a ferment of endless curiosity. The new baby slept seraphically in his cradle.

Penelope knew how lucky she was to have this second family without losing the first. Letty and Essex were growing up into charming companions; she would see them soon, when she returned to Rich's house at Stratford, as well as her three school-boys, Robert and Harry and Charles. Her elder sons and daughters adored her, in spite of everything. All her nine children still belonged to her; she was getting the best of both worlds.

The only cloud on the horizon was the news from Ireland, and that was not bad so much as mysterious. Robin had gone over breathing fire and slaughter against the rebels, with orders to march north immediately and attack Tyrone. When he arrived in Dublin, he changed his plans and set off instead on a rambling journey through the south. The campaigning season slipped away, the troops fell sick, yet nothing was done. The Queen said acidly that she was spending a great deal of money for the Lord Deputy to go on progresses. There was no clue to his motive; in another general, it might have been taken for cowardice or lethargy, but even his sternest critics did not accuse Essex of these failings. His friends could only muzzle their anxiety and wait for better things.

One afternoon in June, Penelope and Charles went to a play at the Globe. Sitting in the Lords' Room, conventionally masked, she looked down into the sunlit circle of the theatre, and saw the platform stage transformed, by the marvellous alchemy of words, to the field of Agincourt. The author of the piece was playing the part of Chorus. She was very interested in that modest young man with the high forehead and the calm air of speculation. Besides being an excellent dramatist, the butcher's son from the Midlands was the only sonnet-writer who had ever outshone Philip Sidney.

Henry V was enthralling, especially to Penelope, who was so reminded of her brother. It was not, of course, a portrait; writers of Shakespeare's calibre did not work in that way. Rather, he had created a character which would satisfy an audience who took their ideal of heroic virtue from the Earl of Essex. The valour and the simplicity, the passionate love for England, all were there. And most endearing, the scene between the King and the soldiers. 'A little touch of Harry in the night' might well have been a little touch of Robin.

When the performance was over, Shakespeare came up to pay his respects to Lord Mountjoy, the close friend of his patron, Lord Southampton.

Charles, who loved the theatre, always enjoyed talking to players.

"This is as nearly faultless as anything you've done," he said. "Though Lady Rich hoped the King would relent towards Falstaff. I'm sorry you've killed the old ruffian."

"I had to be rid of him, my lord. There was no place for him here."

"A pity. Did you know that Her Majesty is most distressed? She wants you to revive him."

Penelope saw in Shakespeare's eyes the hunted expression of an author whose fantasies have got out of control and become common property. She intervened tactfully:

"There was a mention of my brother in a passage you spoke yourself, concerning the King's return. Would you repeat it for me?"

"Gladly, my lady. I hope my prophecy may soon he fulfilled." He quoted, in his low and pleasant voice:

" . . . But now behold,
In the quick forge and working-house
   of thought,
How London doth pour out her
   citizens.
The Mayor and all his brethren in
   best sort,
Like to the Senators of th'antique
   Rome,
With the plebeians swarming at their
   heels,
Go out and fetch their conquering
   Caesar in.
As by a lower but loving likelihood,
Were now the General of our gracious
   Empress,
As in good time he may, from Ireland
   coming,
Bringing rebellion broached on his
   sword,

How many would the peaceful city
  leave
To welcome him."

"I thank you," she said, imagination kindling.

The play had made a deep impression on her, and some fragments of it stuck in her mind, as Shakespeare's lines were apt to do. After supper that evening, she found one of them haunting her. "If it be a sin to covet honour, I am the most offending soul alive." Could it be a sin to crave for something intrinsically good? She consulted Charles.

He thought it over. "Honour can hold no taint of evil; that would be a contradiction in terms. I wonder if the threat lies in the word covet, a greed for something that is not ours to possess. 'A sin to covet honour'. Might there not be a man so intensely in love with his country that he aspired to a destiny for which he was not endowed? A great military career, for instance. That would be a sin of presumption, an attempt to defy the limits that God had set on his nature and destiny."

It seemed a satisfactory answer, and one that had no personal application, for the heroics of the afternoon had left her in an exultant mood, safe from any uncomfortable doubts about what Robin was doing in Ireland, or why Charles had once called him a bad general. Some day he would have his Agincourt.

Part Three

The Fall of Icarus

September 1599 – July 1600

1

ALL through the summer the Irish campaign hung fire, while increasingly bitter and recriminating letters went back and forth between the Queen and her Lord Deputy. At last, in September, he went North in search of Tyrone. But not to fight him. He met the rebel leader by arrangement, at the Ford of Bellaclynthe, and after an hour's parley they concluded a truce.

When this extraordinary news reached England, the Queen's fury fairly blistered the paper of her next despatch. Essex must have guessed how she would take it; he did not wait for the mail, but dashed over from Ireland to defend his actions in person. He reached the Court at Nonsuch very early on the 27th September; finding no one to stop him in the public rooms, he thrust his way into the Queen's bedchamber, where her women were helping her to dress.

"It's unthinkable," exclaimed Penelope, "that any man should invade Her Majesty's privacy in such a manner — even Essex."

She herself had just finished dressing in her lodging; she gazed at Charles and Rich who had brought her the news. They had arrived together, and they were all too preoccupied to find anything incongruous in the situation.

"How did the Queen deal with this visitation?"

"She was delighted to see him," replied Rich. "Or so it seems. Mountjoy can tell you more than I."

Charles said, "They told me he had arrived; I caught him just as he came from her presence. He was well content with his reception, and asked for you immediately."

Penelope got up, shaking out the heavy folds of her velvet skirt, and adjusting her topaz chain. "My fan, Mary." She looked automatically in the glass, hardly conscious of the beautiful reflection of Lady Rich accoutred for the day.

They emerged into the gallery, which was full of hurrying figures and wild speculation. The whole Court seemed to have gone mad.

"Easy to see Robin's back," commented Penelope. "He soon turns the place upside down. Tell me more of their encounter — was she wearing her wig?"

"For heaven's sake, guard your tongue!" snapped Rich.

He need not have worried. That irreverent question was flying round the Palace. The Maids of Honour could supply the answer: when the Earl marched in, the Queen had been wigless and unprotected, an old woman with a thin scrape of hair dangling round her ears.

There was a cluster of people at the door of Robin's lodging, who parted to let them through. Inside the ante-chamber the favoured friends. Among the sybarites in their fragile ruffs and sleek, padded doublets, Robin stood out with a bleak austerity in his soldier's dress, with a plain collar, and his high boots caked with dust. Had he really gone to the Queen like that? Perhaps the Queen had not cared, any more than Penelope did, concentrating on his face. She was shocked to see how thin and white he was, and though he was smiling, his eye-sockets were grooved with pain.

She hid her dismay. "Welcome home, my dear lord."

"My sweet sister!" He hugged her without ceremony. "Can you give me any word of Frank? I had no leisure to enquire in London."

"She's in good heart, though weary of her load. You know the child is due next week."

"Please God this one will live." He turned to Rich. "How glad I am to see you, my dear fellow. You can all guess why I have come — I could not continue over there with nothing to sustain me but harsh abuse from the one being who has most cause to trust me. I'm perfectly aware who are my enemies, and how they have poisoned Her Majesty's mind by wilfully disparaging everything I do. Now that I have free access to her again, I shall soon win back her approval."

There was no time for discussion. He had to change and go to the Queen for a formal audience. Superb, this time, in scarlet and black, and glittering with gold thread. The result was a triumph, proving to Robin what he had always maintained: however much they quarrelled on paper, or in the disrupting company of rival politicians, once they were alone together, he could handle the Queen. Her deep love for him would bridge all their difficulties.

The lords and gentlemen of his faction dined at his table in the hall, and most of the other courtiers came over with cordial greetings.

At one table, the diners sat aloof and grim. These were his opponents, declaring themselves plainly. Cecil, Nottingham, Tom Howard and Ralegh, with their various satellites. Their motives were various and dubious. The Howards were probably honest in their dislike of the favourite's high-handed attitude towards the Queen. The others were thinking less of the Queen than of the future. All Court intrigues, from now on, would pivot on one vital point — who was going to dominate England at the moment of her death? Until recently, Essex had seemed too powerful to challenge, but his Irish adventures might provide a useful weapon for other men with other ideas.

That evening Essex was alone with the

Queen for two hours. No one would ever know what happened; only that the old magic failed him. The next morning he was ordered to stay in his room, while Cecil summoned an emergency meeting of the Council. They sent for the Lord Deputy and put him through a long inquisition on his conduct of the war and his sudden return. All through Sunday he was shut in his lodging. On Monday, the 1st October, he was taken by coach to York House, the London residence of the Lord Keeper. He was a prisoner.

The blow had fallen so quickly, and it was so devastating no one was quite able to believe it. Essex had weathered so many stormy episodes, including that scene last year when he had tried to draw his sword — why should he be arrested now, simply for failing to crush the Irish rebellion? None of his predecessors had done any better.

Gradually Penelope began to see exactly where her brother's heedless independence had landed him. He had disobeyed his orders by frittering away the summer in Southern Ireland, instead of attacking Tyrone. He had made a truce with the rebel general for which he had no sanction whatever. He had conferred knighthoods on a great many of his followers without permission. He had disobeyed the Queen's express command by leaving his post and coming back to England. Finally, he had forced his way into her bedchamber — so typical of Robin, to forget every rule of correct behaviour in his desire to explain himself to the woman who had always loved him. The very fact of that strange and ambiguous love made the matter more delicate: the Virgin Queen was sixty-six, her favourite not yet thirty-two, and the impression of insolent familiarity was particularly disagreeable.

"At least she knows the kind of innocence that prompted him," Penelope said to Rich, as their coach rolled up the road from Surrey. "Poor Robin, he is a perfect fool at times. But surely she need not have put him in prison."

"More likely it's the Irish business that sticks in her gullet," said Rich. "All that vast expense for nothing."

Robin's friends moved into London with an instinct to be near him. They congregated at Essex House, where

Frank's baby girl had been born the previous day. Her eldest child, Philip Sidney's daughter Elizabeth Rutland, was acting as hostess in her stepfather's house. A bride of fifteen, she was in love with the boy Essex had chosen for her, and whom he treated like a son — now her domestic happiness, like her mother's, was spoilt. The Essex party gathered, and talked round the clock: the Southamptons, the Riches, the Rutlands, the Blounts, and the lesser lights — Sir Gelly Meyrick, Essex's steward, Henry Cuffe, the most able of his secretaries, and Anthony Bacon, who was busy drafting letters to the Kings of France and Scotland (Francis Bacon kept cautiously out of the way).

The endless weighing of details and uncertainties led nowhere, and they turned to the friends who streamed into Essex House to show their sympathy. Those who came from the Court were eagerly questioned. Was the Queen really so enraged or was this just a parade of indignation, forced on her by the Council?

"There's no loophole there, I fear," said John Harrington. He was one of

Essex's Irish Knights, and also the Queen's godson; a lively young man with very black, peaked eyebrows and a gift for self-mockery. "I've never seen Her Majesty in such an ill humour. When I plucked up courage to show myself, she blazed out at me, 'What, did the fool bring you too?' As though I and my knighthood were the last straw. And then she must go through the whole history of the expedition; by the time she dismissed me, I was quite undone. I couldn't have run faster if Tyrone and all his rebels had been at my heels."

"Tell us more, Jack," said Southampton. "How did she speak of his lordship?"

"She said we were all idle knaves, and the Lord Deputy worse." Harrington hesitated. "She stamped her foot and swore, 'God's death, that man is above me! Who gave him leave to come here?' That's the crux of it, my lord. She thinks he makes himself too mighty for a subject."

It was a disquieting thought.

Though Robin, from all they could hear, was anything but aggressive. The Council's catalogue of his sins had possibly shaken him as badly as his imprisonment. Until now, no one had ever made him understand that a pure and disinterested patriotism did not entitle him to over-rule the Queen's decisions, however good his intentions. In defying her, he had ignored one essential fact: she was the Lord's Anointed, and her will was sacred. Contrite, he had written her a letter which began *Receive, I humbly beseech Your Majesty, the unfeigned submission of the saddest soul on earth. I have offended in presumption* ... He had never admitted so much before, and that confession alone might have made her forgive him. Unfortunately, she was still far too angry.

She had him closely guarded, would not let him see his friends or write to his wife, and her rancour was increased by the behaviour of her people, who took Essex's troubles as a personal disaster and stood in mournful groups, gazing up at the windows of York House. A little further down the river the visitors to Essex House arrived in such numbers that they turned life there into a kind of macabre and perpetual party.

Penelope was obsessed by her anxiety for Robin, his wretchedness ached like a bruise in her mind. In spite of this, she could not avoid being the centre of all the sympathetic excitement. Her miniature court was annoying the Queen so much that both Charles and Rich told her she would be wise to leave London and rusticate for a while. Grumbling, she went down to Wanstead, taking Bess Southampton with her.

A week dragged by. The news from London grew more ominous, though Penelope did not realise how bad things were until Charles rode down one afternoon to see her, and announced, in his cool undramatic way, that he was planning to rescue Robin from his prison and get him across to France.

"The French King will be glad to give him sanctuary. Or if he doesn't care to leave the country I'll take him to Wales; his tenants there can keep him safe hidden in the mountains."

"Is it so desperate?" she asked, appalled. "Surely this fall from grace can have no lasting effect? Her Majesty has always been so lenient . . . "

"That's it, Penelope. Twelve years of incredible leniency, and now she is set against him. There must be some powerful force behind the scenes to work so great a change in her. And I think I can guess what it is — a conspiracy, directed from Madrid, to remove Essex for good, because he champions the King of Scots as the rightful heir to the throne."

There was no difficulty in naming the chief conspirator. Robert Cecil.

She thought of the Secretary of State, the civil little hunchback, constantly beside the Queen with his feather-light insinuations. He had access to every secret document, every Government agent. A very clever little man, and perhaps a very dangerous one.

Robin had begun to distrust his loyalty before he went to Ireland. Doubt had hardened into certainty. During a long talk with Charles on the day of his return, his last day at liberty, he had said that Cecil was working against him all through the campaign. Cecil had established far too strong an influence over the ageing Queen; if they were not careful, he would

146

betray them all and sell their country into slavery.

"I wasn't entirely convinced at the time," admitted Charles, "but I have been considering all Robert's arguments, and I must say the present circumstances seem to bear them out. And there are so many stories of Cecil's perfidy flying around, they can't all be lies. One thing I'm sure of: if he is a traitor in Spanish pay, he'll have no mercy to spare for Robert. He'll use any means he can to encompass his utter ruin, perhaps his death. We can't leave Robert in the trap as a bait to test Cecil's honesty. That's why I want to get him away."

A messenger was smuggled into York House with details of Charles's plan. He brought back an answer. The Earl was deeply moved by Lord Mountjoy's devotion, but as a loyal subject he could accept his freedom only from the Queen. Nothing would induce him to run away.

It was just as well that Robin refused to be rescued, for in fact he was in no condition to make a hard journey as a fugitive. They had known all along that he was not well, assuming that he had the usual ague and headaches. Mental strain always played havoc with his precarious health. Now the Lord Keeper reported that his prisoner was suffering from the most violent form of Irish dysentery, the horrible disease that had killed his father.

The political implications faded. Robin's life was in danger from an even more insidious enemy than Robert Cecil. Penelope was frantic. She wanted to go to him, to nurse him, and was faced by a brutal restriction. None of his family could get inside York House. Someone would have to put their case to the Queen. Frank, the obvious person, was unwelcome at Court; Robin's sisters might do better. It took the Queen ten maddening days to agree that she would grant an audience to either Lady Rich or Lady Northumberland.

Kneeling in the Privy Chamber, modulating her voice till it was honey-sweet and respectful, Penelope struggled to penetrate the barrier that the Queen had built between herself and her Devereux cousins.

"Madam, I know how gravely he has

offended you — I don't ask Your Majesty to overlook his errors, only that you should temper justice with mercy. He's a sick man."

"Essex has the gift of falling sick whenever it suits his convenience," said the Queen. "Did you never hear the story of the boy who cried Wolf?"

She was stabbing the needle through her embroidery with an irritable hand. The paint had set in rigid lines on her white face, cancelling any hint of feeling. Everything about her today had a shallow, unyielding brightness: the orange wig, the jewelled points of her ruff, the sharp, polished fingernails.

Penelope tried again. "If Essex has succumbed before to Your Majesty's displeasure, it surely proves how vulnerable his love for you has made him. And this distemper is of a different nature. The Lord Keeper has no doubt that he is very ill. May I remind Your Majesty, with all humility, how matters stand at York House? Lady Egerton is ill herself, and the charge of the household and both invalids have fallen on her niece, a girl of sixteen. Could not some older woman be sent to her assistance? I or my sister — unless Your Majesty would permit Lady Essex to go? Your granting such a comfort to an unhappy prisoner would be seen everywhere as a most royal act of clemency."

"No, it wouldn't," snapped the Queen. "It would be seen as an act of wavering infirmity."

She had risen, and was walking up and down the room with quick nervous movements. Penelope watched her. She did understand part of the Queen's dilemma. Twice in the past two years she and her most illustrious subject had quarrelled themselves into a paralysing impasse, and each time it was the Queen who had given way, restoring the favourite to even greater honours and privileges. Of course everyone in the country knew it, which must be galling to the old autocrat. Now she was steeling herself against the smallest show of mercy, because it would be seized on as the start of one more chapter of appeasement, one more sign of her doting infatuation for Essex. Penelope wondered if this was the real reason for her new severity. Whether Robin's supporters were being a little too astute in filling the background with Spanish bribery and sinister plots. Perhaps it took a woman to unravel the agonised and spiteful twistings of another woman who was humiliated by her lonely hunger for affection? The hunger must still be there, and it would save the situation, provided the Queen could appreciate that Robin was really ill.

"Your Majesty's physician has seen my brother," said Penelope, shifting slightly to ease the weight on her knees. "Didn't Dr. Brown tell you how he is decimated by this foul disease? I trust Your Majesty will forgive my harping on it; I can't forget that my father died from the same cause."

"God's wounds, do you think that I forget your father?" The Queen flung round, and Penelope found herself raked by a broadside of genuine Tudor flame. "He was the most noble and faithful servant I ever had. If he were alive today, do you think he would be proud of his son? A renegade who parleys with insurgents? Your father would have turned him out of doors."

Penelope dared not argue. The Queen went storming on in that rough, harsh voice. "He's in good hands with the Lord Keeper — lucky for him he's not in the Tower, as he deserves. Arrogant — ungrateful — contemptuous of our dignity and our authority. He won't be taught by kindness. Very well, then. He must learn his lesson through penance and punishment. It's not yet too late."

Not too late — when he might be on his deathbed. We shall never see him again, thought Penelope, in despair. She knew she had lost, and there was nothing more to be said.

On the 25th November Frank went to Court and tried to see the Queen. It was a forlorn hope, for a favourite's wife was always liable to do more harm than good, but Frank had reached the stage when she must take some sort of action, and the Queen was occasionally touched by an unlikely gesture, particularly if it had needed a good deal of courage. Penelope was again at Essex House. When her sister-in-law returned, one glance was enough to tell her that she had failed.

"I didn't see her." Frank came slowly

to the fire, shivering. She was dressed in symbolic black, without a single ornament. That, and her sleepless nights, had dimmed her lustre; she looked pinched and plain. "They wouldn't even tell her I was there, Pen. Our own friends were afraid to talk to me, in case they should be dragged into our troubles. They told me to go away. It was horrible."

It was the way of courts. Those people, who had been competing for invitations from the Earl and Countess of Essex a few months ago, had neither the guts nor the grace to comfort a woman whose husband was probably dying. Penelope could picture their annoyance at being pestered, and the patronising stares and whispers of some of the pampered girls who had been Robin's mistresses. It was shaming that Frank, with her gentle integrity, should be exposed to such a crew.

Frank knelt down by the fire. "They say he's weaker. I stopped at York House to enquire. I think I shall go out of my mind — how can I endure this for the second time?"

Penelope took a moment to grasp what

153

she meant by the second time.

"Out there at Arnhem," whispered Frank. "When Philip was lying wounded, I thought it was the hardest of all fates, to see my beloved husband die before my eyes. I didn't know — oh I didn't know! The torment of being shut out when Robin is so close, when he may be calling for me through the fever, alone and friendless."

She began to cry. Penelope sat on the floor and slipped an arm round her shoulders, offering the shelter and warmth she would have given to one of her own children, while Frank wept in the unpractised, choking way of someone too reserved to find tears easy.

"I love him so," she said, when she grew calmer. "He has his faults, my sweet Robin. I was never blind to any of them, and what do they matter? He's the light of my days. If he should die in prison — he told me once how he dreads the pangs of death. (They don't think of that, because he is so valiant.) If it pleases God to take him, I only want to be with him to the end, to help my darling through the last narrow gate. Is that so great a thing to ask?"

"It's a monstrous thing to refuse," said Penelope.

Curiously, Frank's grief upset her more than the actual knowledge of Robin's sufferings. Frank's love was so completely good and selfless — though she had certainly had as much to forgive as the Queen, one way and another. To deny such love its final expression was an outrage against Christian charity; it seemed incredible that any woman could be so tyranically cruel.

I hate her, thought Penelope. Something in her heart had perished, the mystical allegiance of a lifetime was gone, leaving her with a fierce and bitter loathing for the Queen.

Robin's case was brought before the Star Chamber in his absence, and he was severely censured for his conduct of the war in Ireland, and for his unauthorised return. The immediate purpose of this was to justify the Queen's treatment of her Lord Deputy, so that all his misdemeanours could be trotted out for the edification of the English people, who paid no attention and remained obstinately loyal to their hero.

The next day there was a sudden gleam of expectation, when the Queen paid a surprise visit to York House, and saw the patient, who was too hard-pressed to know that she was there, his eyes closed in a stupor of exhaustion. She surveyed him in silence, and then she went away. She made no concession to his wife or sisters.

"No doubt she satisfied herself that he was play-acting," said Penelope, with a savage astringency.

By the 10th December Robin had been a prisoner for seventy-one days, ailing all the time, and dangerously ill for six weeks. It seemed that the end was very near, and that Sunday morning the churches throughout London offered prayers to God for His servant Robert. There was nothing organised in this, it was entirely spontaneous.

That afternoon at Essex House they waited in the gallery, helpless and idle. Henry Wotton, one of the junior secretaries, came to the door and signalled to Charles, who got up and went out.

Penelope put down the book she was not reading, and followed him, in time to catch what Wotton was saying.

"I thought I ought to warn your lordship that the church bells are tolling all along the Strand."

"He can't be dead!" exclaimed Penelope. "I don't believe it. The Lord Keeper would have sent us word."

"I'll go to York House myself," said Charles. "You come with me, Henry; the secretary there is a friend of yours. No need to inform the Countess until we discover the truth."

Penelope insisted on joining them. They made the short trip by water; the lavender grey London haze was already deepening into a winter night, the river was deserted and forlorn and the familiar places merely bulks of shadow as they passed: Arundel House, Somerset House, the Savoy, Durham House. Faintly across their rooftops came that dreadful tolling of the bells.

They pulled alongside a private landing-stage. Wotton got out; after a slight altercation, he was allowed inside the house to find his friend. Penelope and

157

Charles were admitted to a small porter's lodge; it was as far as they could go.

Presently Wotton reappeared with two companions. "It's a false alarm," he said at once. "The Earl's condition is unchanged. May I present Mrs. Ann More to your ladyship. And Mr. John Donne."

"Unchanged?" Penelope looked critically at the Lord Keeper's beautiful little niece, who swept her a curtsy. The child's no older than Letty, she thought, distrusting that soft immaturity. "Do you mean he is no worse?"

John Donne, the Lord Keeper's secretary, answered her. "I fear he is no better, madam. He received the Sacrament this morning, since when he has been wonderfully peaceful."

Which sounded like a death-warrant. Penelope bit her lip. To beg for news from strangers, when Robin was upstairs in the same house and slipping away from her for ever. It was unnatural, intolerable.

"If only I could see him!" she burst out.

There was an uncomfortable pause. Though the Lord Keeper himself was not hostile, they all knew there would be spies about the place, ready to run to Cecil. Even this conference must be a secret.

Charles put a steadying hand on her arm. "We dare not increase Her Majesty's displeasure."

"What can that signify, when he's at the point of death?"

"I think he's going to live," said Ann More, speaking for the first time in a surprisingly firm tone. Penelope looked at her again.

"I do," persisted the girl. "His lordship thinks himself that he is dying; that's because he can't remember how ill he was last week. He's worn to the edge of his endurance, but the fever is abated, and the pain much less. My lady, I wish we could take you to him, so that you could judge. You must consider me quite unequal to the care of such a patient, though I promise you we are all doing our best."

"Mrs. More is a most skilful nurse," said Donne, moving protectively closer to her.

"I'm sure she is." Unexpectedly, Penelope

was sure. "Does he ask for any of us, my dear?"

"Not when he is conscious; he understands why it is that you may not come. He talks of his faith in God. And of Her Majesty. When his mind wanders, I have heard him say your name, and if I bathe his forehead, he will murmur 'Frank' in so loving a voice — is that what he calls Lady Essex?"

"Yes. I'll tell her. She will be as grateful as I am, for all you are doing to save my brother. You have given me hope — though I suppose I must not let it grow too high."

"Any other man would have died a week ago," said Donne. "His lordship has more grip on life than most of us. He could always perform amazing feats of strength."

He spoke with a reminiscent admiration, and Penelope, observing him more carefully, thought the Lord Keeper's secretary had a vivid and exciting quality about him, suggesting a varied experience.

"Did you know Lord Essex before?" she asked.

"Mr. Donne served under him in the

160

Islands," Charles told her. "And also at Cadiz."

Cadiz. The name evoked such glory; how happy, how proud of Robin, they had been, just over three years ago. The contrast was too tragic. Penelope was on the verge of breaking down. Charles, watching her, said they must not delay Mrs. More any longer. He helped Penelope through the civilities and then, with an infinite tenderness, guided her down the slippery steps to the boat.

Convinced that he would not live through the night, Robin had asked that the patents of his various State appointments should be returned to the Queen. This did jolt her out of her indifference. She sent the patents back to him — as though forbidding him to die — ordered eight doctors to York House immediately, and admitted at last that the proper person to look after Essex was his wife.

Frank was on her way ten minutes after the Queen's message arrived. The first sight of Robin would be an ordeal, but she was well prepared. She had seen Sidney die, and her father, and two of her little sons. Robin, she told Penelope that evening, was no worse than she had imagined. He was so pitifully weak that when they made his bed, they had to lift him in the sheet; however, Ann More was right, the disease had run its course, and his weakness was the real adversary now. That was something they could fight. He still had a chance.

Penelope went to Court again, and begged for permission to help with the nursing. This was refused, although the Queen was in a much more gracious mood, and there were tears in her eyes when she spoke of Robin.

"I have been so greatly distressed by what the doctors tell me. Indeed, when I think of him in the full power of his health, the many pleasant hours we have enjoyed . . . "

There was a catch in her throat, she stared towards the door, as though she half hoped to see her tall young favourite come swinging through with his refreshingly direct manner and the innate charm which fascinated all women and most men. His fire of enthusiasm, his physical splendour, the echo of his laughter haunted the Palace.

"We must thank God that he begins to mend," said the Queen more briskly. "I trust he may profit from his afflictions, my poor Essex. His spirit is true, I've never doubted that, and he has so many surpassing virtues, despite the faults he inherits from your mother. He must be prevented, at all costs, from repeating those sins which have brought him down. Remember this, Penelope: whatever I do, it is for his salvation. To school him, not to destroy him."

Once Penelope would have melted to that affectionate concern. Now she listened cynically, and wondered what complacent visions of her own righteousness were passing through the old woman's mind. The last month had left its mark on Penelope, and her response to the world was changing.

Frank went every morning to York House and came home more cheerful every night. Robin had stopped being saintly and was getting rather fractious; it was an excellent sign. By Christmas he was well on the road to recovery.

2

WHILE Robin was so desperately ill, nothing else had mattered, the world had seemed to stand still. But of course the world never did stand still; the Irish truce was over, and the cunning Hugh O'Neill, Earl of Tyrone, had not wasted his advantage. By January the whole of Ireland outside the Pale was in a ferment. It was imperative to appoint a new Lord Deputy, and this time the Queen was going to make her own choice; she was determined to send Lord Mountjoy.

"There's no escape," said Charles. "I couldn't wriggle free from it, try how I might." He had just come from a session with the Queen and Council. "I told them that I was unworthy of so great a place, that they needed a more experienced commander to succeed where Essex had failed. I even told them that Essex's wretched plight was bound to discourage any aspiring general. Her

164

Majesty merely said that a general who obeys orders has nothing to fear from her, a statement few would agree with. Then I tried another tack; said it would be most unfitting that I should profit by the disgrace of a friend who was united to me by close family ties. She gave me her haughtiest stare, and asked 'What family ties?' So I replied, 'Your Majesty will recall that the Earl's stepfather is my cousin.' I wish you could have seen her face. She said, 'Mountjoy, you're as glib as any of my Irish subjects. Go and rule them for me.' With much more of my duty to God and to her, until I could not honourably decline. I'm sorry, Penelope."

"Duty to God!" snapped Penelope. "Does He require that you should be thrown to the wolves? It's outrageous — why must she send all the men I love to that filthy island of savages? How can I bear to let you go, knowing what Ireland did to my father and brother?"

"We must pray that I may be more fortunate."

"Yes. To be sure. I shall pray for you continually."

"But with no great conviction, I take it?" Charles eyed her thoughtfully, and said, without the smallest rancour, "The trouble is, you don't think me a good enough soldier."

She was in a quandary. They never alluded to that occasion when Charles had insisted that Robin's failure in the Azores was due to military incompetence. If there were times when this seemed the most likely explanation of his curious behaviour in Ireland, Charles was too loyal, and far too kind, to crow. And Penelope could not quite accept that verdict. Robin might not be another Hannibal; at least he was a professional soldier, as capable as any they had, with the kind of magnetism that inspired large assemblies of men to the point of idolatry.

Charles had none of these gifts. Dearly as she loved him, she knew he did not show at his best among strangers, who were apt to be chilled by his reserve and his air of languor. Besides, it was one thing to criticise, quite another to command. Charles's idea of strategy was theoretical; as Robin had said, he was too bookish. But she could not possibly hurt him by giving her true opinion.

All this ran through her brain, very quickly, before she answered. "I don't under-rate your merits, dear heart — never think that. I doubt we have anywhere a soldier good enough to subjugate the Irish. Through Her Majesty's whole reign they've been our plague, and of all the wise and valiant governors who've been sent over there, each came home poorer in health, wealth and reputation. Oh, I know some unlucky devil must take over Robin's office, but why did it have to be you?"

Charles shrugged. "That's the penalty for public service. I never took less pleasure in the sweet sound of 'Friend, go up higher'. Though the Irish pitfalls daunt me less than the thought of leaving England, deserting Robert when he needs every support we can give him."

They were all weighed down by the same uneasy foreboding. Robin had been a prisoner in York House for nearly fourteen weeks. His followers were certain that someone was poisoning the Queen's mind with insinuations against her favourite.

Someone whose identity was never in doubt.

"I wish you could move Her Majesty's clemency towards my brother, Mr. Secretary," Penelope said to this person a few days later, testing him out. They were strolling in the long gallery at Whitehall on a wet January afternoon.

"Indeed, I have tried continually, Lady Rich." Sir Robert Cecil gazed up at her with his rather mournful eyes. "I have been a constant advocate for his lordship; I don't forget his many kindnesses, nor the warm regard there used to be between us, though I fear he has come to distrust me."

"I wonder why that should be?"

"It's because I want to end the war with Spain. We may disagree over public affairs, yet I would gladly be the instrument of obtaining his freedom, so that we could become private friends once more. I'm doing all I can."

Penelope was baffled. The little man didn't seem like a villain when you were with him. Another minute and they would be lapsing into the habit of years, exchanging jokes and confidences about their fellow-courtiers. Suspicion died in such a climate of comfortable intimacy.

This mood did not last long. Penelope still could not get permission to visit Robin, and she blamed Cecil for the delay. Tired of trying to get into York House, she and her sister Dorothy and the Southamptons persuaded the Lord Keeper's next-door neighbour to let them go into his garden, so that they could talk to Robin over the wall when he came out for his morning walk.

It was a painful encounter. Robin's normal distinguished pallor was spectral, his features drawn to the bone, and his greeting to his sisters was defensive and half-ashamed. It had not struck Penelope that when a great man fell from power, his own family might be the last people he wanted to see.

He reached across the wall to touch their hands, and repeated their names, Pen and Doll, as he had called them ever since they were children. Then, like fools, they could none of them think what to say.

Southampton enquired if there was anything they could do for him.

"Can you do anything for those miserable caged lions at the Tower?" enquired Robin bitterly, as he dragged his cloak around him and shivered in the winter desolation.

Making an effort, he said that he would be glad of some more books, otherwise he was well cared for, and having Frank with him was an untold blessing. They talked of his children. Young Robert had gone back to Eton after the Christmas holiday; it was nearly a year since his father had seen him, and the new baby, little Lady Frances Devereux, he had never seen at all.

"Frank tells me she takes after you, Pen, so I've sired a beauty."

Towards the end, he spoke of his continued disgrace; he was convinced that all would be put right if only he could see the Queen.

"You must petition to get me a private audience," he told Penelope. "And try if you can discover what has kept me out of her presence so long. What secret doubt or grudge can have inflamed her anger to such a degree? I have committed certain follies, for which I've humbled myself and begged for mercy — what more does she require? Left to herself she would never refuse me access; it's Cecil's doing, I'm sure of that. Pen, you must find out what slanders he has invented, so I may answer them."

Penelope promised to do her best. She attended the Court next day. The Queen had heard of the assignation at the garden wall — through Cecil's spies, of course — and she was furious. Cecil himself assured Penelope that she would be wise to stay away from the Palace. Penelope thought he was being deliberately obstructive, not to say two-faced, and she went home in a rage.

She needed Charles to smooth down her spiky animosity; unfortunately, he was busy equipping himself and his staff for his campaign, surrounded by armourers, victuallers and farriers, and constantly attended by his sergeant-major-general. Having realised that Charles had got to go to Ireland, Penelope was keeping up a brave façade, but she dreaded their approaching separation, and this dread, as well as Cecil's perfidy, plunged her into a restless activity. She had got to do something drastic.

Still boiling with indignation, she worked out a plan. She would write to the Queen, pleading for the audience that Robin wanted so badly, but also taking the opportunity to tell Her Majesty a few home truths — that she had delegated too many decisions to the Secretary of State, that he and his satellites were keeping her effectively cut off from all her honest statesmen, while plotting the ruin of Essex, and furthering their own guilty ambitions, until the inevitable time must come when she would find herself alone and powerless to control them. No actual names need be mentioned, the meaning would be plain. The form, on the other hand, must be excessively ornate, decorated with every fulsome turn of flattery that would appeal to the Queen. Penelope sat down at her table, and began to write.

Early did I hope this morning to have mine eyes blessed with Your Majesty's beauties, but seeing the sun disappear into a cloud, and meeting with spirits that did presage, by the wheels of their chariots, some thunder in the air, I must complain and express my fears to the High Majesty and Divine Oracle, unto whose powers I must sacrifice again and again the tears and prayers of the afflicted — She paused, nibbling her quill. This sentence was getting rather involved; it was a marvellous counterfeit of that sickening adulation which the Queen liked to wallow in. Penelope went on, writing with passion of *my unfortunate brother, whom all have liberty to defame*, and of his enemies glutting themselves in their unbridled hate. *Such crafty workmen as will not only pull down all obstacles to their greatness, but when they are in their full strength (like giants) make war on Heaven.* That was sufficiently blunt; it must be offset by tributes to Her Majesty's wisdom, unstained virtue and compassion. She closed with a suitable flourish: *I presume to kiss your fairest hands, vowing all obedience and endless love.*

Had she spread the butter too thick? Impossible, the old woman was blinded by vanity. Penelope was not so simple that she thought her appeal would succeed directly. There was about one chance in ten that Robin might get his audience;

more likely the Queen would be very much annoyed, but Penelope did not care. Her aim was to phrase her barbed hints in exactly the way to discredit Cecil. The Queen would not relish the thought that he and Ralegh were using her as a dupe, and that the whole country knew it.

Penelope copied out her letter, and despatched it before she lost her nerve. Because the excitements of literary composition had gone to her head a little, she showed the rough draft about among her friends, who found it hugely entertaining.

Charles was not entertained. He was horrified.

"You should never have sent it — Can't you see how it will provoke her wrath?"

"Because I implied that she is Cecil's puppet?"

"I meant your manner of addressing her. You must know that you've been extremely impertinent."

"But Charles, everyone writes to her in that odious fashion."

"Every man may, it's part of a courtly conceit which she understands better than you think. Women have no place in that pattern, you least of all. Do use your wits, Penelope. You're thirty years younger than she is, you've been the most famous beauty in England all your life, and are still unrivalled, because you do in fact possess that perfection of face and body which we ascribe to the Queen. How do you think she'll read those outrageous compliments, from such a one as you?"

"I hope she'll lap them up," said Penelope, stifling some faint qualms. She had not seen the matter in this light, and was not going to fret about it now, being more concerned in noticing how splendid Charles looked when he was being severe, and how funny he sounded, speaking of her unrivalled perfection in such a cross voice.

When she heard that the Queen had thrown her letter on the fire in a rage, Penelope did feel some inner trepidation, but nothing happened and she soon regained her self-confidence. In the meanwhile, Charles's time was running out. He was immersed in preparations, often anxious and preoccupied.

One evening he arrived at her house in St. Bartholomew's an hour late for supper.

"I was delayed in conference with the Lord Treasurer," he explained, hurrying over a plate of cold capon and a glass of wine. "Unfortunate, because I've asked Southampton and Danvers to meet me here. You don't mind? I thought it would arouse less notice."

There was a bold rap on the front door, and Penelope gave up the prospect of a peaceful evening alone with Charles.

Her guests were ushered in: Harry Southampton, with his golden, if rather empty, good looks, and Sir Charles Danvers, a tough adventurer, who was negotiating some financial business for Essex, and for that reason was one of the very few people who was occasionally allowed to visit him. When they were all seated, Charles astonished Penelope by asking to borrow her Bible. Mystified, she fetched it.

"I am going to swear an oath," said Charles. "And afterwards I shall ask you two gentlemen to do the same." He stood up, taking off his hat, and gripping the Bible in his right hand. "I swear by Almighty God that I will faithfully serve and defend my Sovereign

176

Lady, Queen Elizabeth, and uphold the lawful proceedings of her Council and Parliament, as long as she shall live." He kissed the Book, and handed it to Southampton.

"I don't see the need for this," objected Harry. "However, to please your lordship . . . " He went through the same formula, and Danvers followed him.

Charles sat back in his chair, stretched his long legs, and began to talk. He emphasised the growing fear that Essex was the victim of conspirators who meant to claim the throne for the Spanish Infanta. Essex was not only the chief adherent of her rival, the King of Scots; he was also the one man who was so universally loved and respected that his chosen candidate might be acceptable to all the different groups in the country. Even the Catholics looked hopefully towards him as the champion of religious toleration. There would be little enthusiasm for the Infanta, unless Essex could be put out of the way.

"Which may well be the true cause of his present misfortunes," said Charles. "The trouble is, we can't be sure. We may be wrong about Cecil. It is equally plausible that the Queen is swayed entirely by motives of her own. She is, after all, a lady who has bewildered better minds than ours, these forty years. And if it is her will that Essex should pay a high price for offending her, we can do nothing." There was bound to be some sort of legal enquiry, to satisfy public opinion, and that would clarify the situation. Provided the prosecution arose simply out of the Queen's anger over the Irish business, Essex would be given a just and impartial hearing: at the worst he would probably be banished from the Court and lose his State appointments. "Which would be a hard enough blow," said Charles. "Yet if that's the way it goes, we can comfort ourselves that Cecil and the Spaniards are not in league against him. They would require a more decisive victory."

"Wouldn't they be satisfied, my lord," suggested Danvers, "if he were publicly disgraced and deprived of his offices?"

"Hardly, while there remained a daily risk that the Queen might have a whim to fetch him back again. She's very lonely . . . Even if she left him in the wilderness, he would still cast a long shadow across the future. What will happen when she dies? What would happen if she died tonight? Essex would walk out of York House tomorrow morning, into a City that adores him, and everyone would flock to him for leadership. No. He will be a menace to the Spanish cause until he is either dead, or locked away in some fortress, his reputation blackened beyond repair. You know the only means to those ends. A charge of high treason."

Penelope and Southampton both interrupted to ask what Essex had ever done that could provide his enemies with such a weapon.

"He's been remarkably indiscreet. During that unlucky parley with Tyrone, the two Earls conversed alone, without witnesses. It could be alleged that they came to an agreement: Tyrone to hold Ireland, unmolested, in return for helping Essex to subjugate England. There have been too many wild rumours that Essex means to make himself King; it only needs a judicious amount of false evidence — the sort of evidence that can always be bought by foreign gold, especially from the Irish. So there's your weapon, for Cecil to draw if he chooses. Will he choose? We know that Essex is innocent; if he is charged with treason, we shall know that Cecil is guilty."

They digested this.

"You said once," Penelope reminded him, "that we couldn't leave Essex in the trap as a bait to determine Cecil's honesty."

"We must spring the trap. Here is what I propose. I shall send these conclusions to King James, giving my view that the destruction of Essex would be the opening skirmish in a campaign to deprive His Majesty of his inheritance. I'll suggest a counter-attack. If Essex is arraigned, the King should mass his troops on the Border, and send ambassadors to Whitehall, demanding a formal recognition that he is the heir to the English throne."

"He'll need to send the troops as well as the ambassadors," commented Danvers. "He won't get his recognition by fair words alone — not with Cecil in the saddle here."

"Scottish soldiers in England! That would be fatal," said Penelope. "The people would never forgive him."

"I agree with you both," said Charles. "There must be some show of force, and we can't call in the Scots. The soldiers will be English." He paused. His three companions waited, not knowing what to expect. "If the need arises, I shall bring the Army back from Ireland and march on London."

There was a frozen silence. Penelope felt her muscles tighten. She had a queer sensation of not being able to breathe.

Southampton spoke slowly, with a mixture of awe and apprehension. "That has the savour of armed rebellion, Mountjoy."

"It will be more than a savour if I fail," retorted Charles. "I shall certainly go to the block."

He got up, to throw another log on the fire, and stayed there, tinkering with the poker. They could not see his face. "I have made this resolve after a long searching of my conscience. I know very well that I should be branding myself as a rebel, yet there are times when a man must sacrifice everything, even the semblance of honour, for his country's greater good. It is vital to us all and to our children that the succession be lawfully established; King James is not only the Prince we should prefer — a Protestant neighbour who speaks our own language — he is also the Queen's nearest kinsman and undoubted heir. Never forget that.

"I believe she means to declare for him at last, but who can foretell the hour and manner of her death, or what ascendancy Cecil may obtain over her before the end? I shall never defy her in any other circumstance. I may have to enter her Palace with a regiment of infantry at my heels, arrest her Secretary, intimidate her Council for a day or two — once Essex is set free and King James acknowledged as her heir presumptive, I shall become again her most dutiful subject. Even though she hates me ever after."

There was no colour of emotion in the level voice; surely no one could ever have planned an act of military coercion with so little bravado or thought of personal glory. Charles's perception of the facts was sharpened, as always, by the cold, clear light of his intellectual integrity.

The other two men were deeply impressed. Southampton said, "If you do come in this warlike manner, I can promise that all your friends here will rally to support you. Danvers and I will see to that; we understand your reasons perfectly."

"Indeed, I hope you do." Charles turned to survey him, his eyes grave and compelling. "I have tried to show you that this whole question of a Spanish plot hangs on the complicity of Cecil. Supposing I brought back the Irish Army, it would be generally believed that my main object was to rescue Essex. But I could do so only in this one instance — if he was the sacrificial victim in a conspiracy that threatened the whole nation. You must make no mistake over this. I cannot come simply to save him from the consequences of having displeased the Queen, no matter what hardships or slights he may suffer at her hands. He is the man I love most in the world, my dear and lifelong friend, the brother of the lady I regard as my wife." There was a brief glance at

Penelope. "However strongly I feel these claims, I could never forget my allegiance or betray my trust by using the forces of the Crown as a lever against Her Majesty in a private quarrel. Danvers, when next you have permission to visit the Earl, you will tell him all I have said this evening; take good care to make this distinction very plain."

Danvers said that the Earl himself would certainly appreciate Lord Mountjoy's scruples. There was a practical discussion of plans and passwords, and the safest way of sending news to Scotland and Ireland. Presently the visitors left.

"Well?" Charles appealed to Penelope. "I hope you approve of my decision? You have not yet told me so."

She was sitting on a wide oak chest, outwardly placid, while her imagination raced. Watching Charles, she could not help studying the strong column of his neck above the ruff. (If I fail, I shall certainly go to the block.) She wrenched her mind away. He was waiting for her answer.

"I'm bound to approve. Some honest man must act, and fate is giving you the opportunity — how I wish it was not so! Charles, I am afraid."

"The hornets' nest may turn out a mare's nest," he said, without much conviction. Now that they were alone, he was no longer the crisp, hard-headed maker of policies. He came round and perched on the chest behind her, drawing her gently back and holding her close for comfort.

"Supposing your endeavour succeeded," she said. "You admit yourself that the Queen might hate you ever after, and I think she would. What then?"

"I should have to go abroad. Would you run away to Scotland with me, Angel? They say Edinburgh's a fine city."

"With you, I'd run away to Babylon. On foot, if need be."

He laughed softly, stroking her hair, and she wondered whether they ought to have seized on this solution right at the beginning, instead of putting up with their curious half-marriage for the sake of her children, his career, their loyalty to Robin — all those other interests which had distracted too much of their attention. Eight years had slipped away unheeded, and now they had only two short weeks before he left her to go into certain danger, possibly to his death.

"Time passes so quickly," she whispered.

"I know," he said, completely understanding. "And you're too brave to squander it on fears and lamentations. Come to bed, sweetheart. I can still teach you to be happy, I promise you."

It was true, she thought later, lying in his arms: when Charles made love to her the sun and moon stood still in the heavens, nothing existed beyond their desire for each other and their constant delight in its accomplishment.

All through that final fortnight she managed to keep up her courage, because he needed her so badly, and because every moment they could be together was too precious to spoil.

He spent his last night with her, and left her at four in the morning. He was due to set out from Holborn at ten, but he did not want Penelope there, a victim for everyone to gape at. So she said goodbye to him in her own doorway, heard his footsteps die away across the paved court of Bart's Priory, and crept upstairs.

Her bedchamber seemed very empty. She blew out the taper and got back into bed. She tried to ward off the invasion of loneliness by pretending that Charles was still beside her; she could hear him breathing, she could reach for his hand in the darkness, and he would wake and turn to her. It was no use. The silence was flat and dead. Charles was not here, and she was suddenly convinced that he would never come to her in this room again. She had a foreboding of tragedy; she had lost her hold on the past. The golden days were over.

3

KNOWING how desolate she would be in the little house that Charles had made alive for her, Penelope moved into Rich's suburban mansion at Stratford-le-Bow, hoping that the bustle of children and servants would help to fill the dreary existence that lay ahead. She had only been there two days when she was jolted out of her boredom.

The original draft of her provocative letter to the Queen had been handed round among her friends, because Penelope's intellectual vanity had been flattered, and she had enjoyed the chorus of admiration, the raised eyebrows and irreverent laughter. She might have guessed what would happen. An unscrupulous printer had got hold of a copy and published it. The sale was enormous. The Queen saw this as a deliberate attempt to excite sympathy for Essex, and Penelope was summoned to appear before the Privy Council.

Now rather alarmed, she took to the courtier's usual refuge. She went to bed and said she was ill.

But she could not stay in bed indefinitely, and the Queen was quite capable of sending a cohort of doctors to examine her. In fact, she sent the Lord Treasurer; it would be wiser to tackle him.

Burleigh's successor, Lord Buckhurst, was a worthy middle-aged peer who had always been charmed by Penelope. He found himself at a disadvantage, trying to deliver a stern reproof to this heavenly creature who challenged his pity with her tragic dark eyes, and murmured that she was so much alone in the world, she had no man to turn to for advice. Her lout of a husband had scurried off to the country. However, she was surrounded by her angelically beautiful children; there was such a tribe of them, it was impossible to remember which were Riches and which were Blounts, and their restless consort of noise and movement drowned any serious conversation. Buckhurst said he wished to speak to her privately, but it seemed that several of the lambs might be sickening with the measles, the doting mother could not let them out of her sight, and her passive repetitions that she was so very sorry to have displeased the Queen were decidedly absent-minded. They were punctuated by the roars of a small boy who looked as though he would get what he wanted in any battle of wits — he was certainly Mountjoy's son. Lord Buckhurst retreated, ruffled, without making any of his weighty speeches.

When he had gone, Penelope picked up Master St. John Blount and danced round the room with him, humming a galliard and laughing. Unfortunately the Queen was not impressed by Buckhurst's account of the interview, and Penelope was again ordered — much more sharply — to present herself before the Council.

In the end she had to go. She was driven to the Palace in her coach; it was disconcerting to find that she was to be ushered into the Council Chamber by the Secretary of State, the anonymous, but easily identified, villain of her letter to the Queen. Cecil looked hurt, rather like a spaniel when you trod on it by mistake, thought Penelope.

"Your ladyship won't take it amiss if I mention that this is an official hearing; their lordships are entitled to a certain degree of submission."

"I think I know how to conduct myself properly, Sir Robert."

She had already decided that submission, of the most feminine and guileless kind, was necessary for Robin's sake, galling as it must be. And here were their lordships at the long table: Buckhurst, Nottingham, the Lord Keeper Egerton, the Archbishop of Canterbury, her uncle Sir William Knollys, and several more. As she approached them she was pleased to observe that the Councillors, who had known her all her life, were extremely uncomfortable.

She was given a chair, which was a concession, and the enquiry began. They were ready to believe that the letter had been published without her consent, and moved on to the next question. What evidence lay behind her hints of treachery, and who had inspired her to make them?

She knew she had no real evidence against Cecil or Ralegh, so she sheltered behind a screen of vague bewilderment.

"It may be that I have exaggerated my random fears. Your lordships will understand how my brother's misfortunes have worked on my mind. I cannot credit that Her Majesty would hold him so long in durance unless he was slandered by his enemies — and hers. As to whom the cap fits, I have not the skill to determine."

Cecil was busy taking notes. He did not look up.

She stuck to her point, and to the truthful statement that she had written the letter entirely on her own initiative. Surely they could not suspect Robin of telling her what to say? She had seen him only once in the last four months, when they had talked for a short time over the Lord Keeper's garden wall.

"And indeed we had other matters to speak of then," she seized on the pathos of that reunion, it was worth stressing. "I gave him news of his children, his little son and the daughter he has not yet been allowed to see."

A hostile Councillor, Lord Shrewsbury, tried another line.

"Did Lord Mountjoy read your letter

before it was sent?"

"Lord Mountjoy? No, my lord. I have told you, I did not consult with any of my acquaintances."

There was a faint, well-bred surprise, as though she barely knew Mountjoy and found the question quite irrelevant. It was the Councillors who were embarrassed, and several mutters of protest were directed at Shrewsbury. Penelope smiled to herself, her eyelids demurely lowered. Their lordships were quite easy to handle, if you had the measure of their weaknesses. Poor creatures, she knew them far too well. They were not a very inspiring lot, wagging their beards and conferring in undertones. There was only one Member of Her Majesty's Most Honourable Privy Council who could impose his will on any company by the sheer fire of his genius, and he was supposed to be so dangerous that he had to be shut up like an animal. The rest, she thought scornfully, were a bunch of mediocrities, puffed out with straw.

Buckhurst addressed her. "We have now concluded our judgment. Your ladyship will stand while you hear it."

There was a change in his manner, and in the general atmosphere. A warning sparked in Penelope's brain, but she got up in a leisurely way and stood in front of the table, composed and graceful.

The Lord Treasurer cleared his throat. "We are satisfied that your written accusations were no more than idle mischief, and also that you wrote without any outside encouragement. Hence there is no need to pursue our investigation. There remains one very grave aspect we have not yet touched on; your impertinence in writing to Her Majesty in such a style. You declared, in so many words, that she was allowing herself to be misled by her servants, and if that were not offensive enough, to so mighty a Prince, you aggravated your fault by displaying, in your pretended courtesy, a wanton impudence of which you should be thoroughly ashamed. I hope you are ashamed, Lady Rich, though you have shown little sign of it. Did you imagine Her Majesty would swallow your brazen taunts, while you mocked at her simplicity?"

Penelope was badly shaken by this

uncompromising harshness from her ally Buckhurst. Her complacency left her, and she flushed, the colour swimming up under the skin, so that it was no good trying to act indifference. Her heart pounding, she stammered an excuse.

"I wrote hastily, not foreseeing how it would be construed . . . "

"You showed a singular lack of perception. It pains me to rebuke you; we are well aware of the anxieties you have endured on your brother's account, yet that is no warrant for *lèse-majesté* and the insolent presumption that I confess I find astonishing in a lady of your noble lineage."

This was horrible, to be publicly scolded for bad manners, and to know that she deserved it. Buckhurst was obviously hating his task, which made it worse; the fact that he felt bound to say these things was an added reproach. Through her confusion, Penelope realised that the others were sharing her discomfort and steadfastly not looking at her. But she realised too that they were united in condemning her, and she had got to make an apology that would placate them. She managed as well as she could, promising to write again to the Queen, in a very different fashion. "And I trust your lordships will assure Her Majesty of my good faith."

"She may find that hard to accept." Penelope's cousin Nottingham, the Lord Admiral, leant on the table, the winter light gleaming cold on his white hair. "You and your brother seem to think you are licensed to behave as you choose, with no respect of persons. You have both been the darlings of fortune; it's high time you learnt that matters of state, and the dignity of your Prince, are not toys for the diversion of spoilt children."

To Penelope, who considered herself an able politician, this was a cruel cut, but somehow all the resistance had gone out of her. The Privy Councillors were no longer comic or negligible. Though they had none of the mystique of awe and ritual that surrounded the Queen, no armoury of shattering Tudor rage, these sedate noblemen, whom Penelope had thought she could lead by the nose, were suddenly brought into a new perspective: they were the executive power through which her country was governed, and they had complete authority to discipline an unruly subject.

She wondered, for the first time, whether she — and Robin — had been breaking the rules of a game they did not properly understand. Their familiar world had become a frightening place, people reacted in such unexpected ways, and she was now assailed by the thought that her mistaken cleverness might bring more trouble to Robin, though he had no part in it. The idea that she might have hurt him reduced her to the status of a beggar.

She appealed to Buckhurst. "My Lord Treasurer, I ask no favours for myself, but I do implore you to use your influence in allaying Her Majesty's anger. I could not bear it if my — my folly was visited on Lord Essex." She despised the tremor of pleading in her voice, but she could not conceal it.

"I will do what I can," said Buckhurst. "In the meantime, I have to inform you of your punishment. It is the Queen's command that you are to return to your own house and remain there as a prisoner until Her Majesty is pleased to pardon your misconduct. Is that clear, Lady Rich?"

"Yes, my lord," whispered Penelope.

She made the required deep curtsy to the Lords of the Council, and prepared to withdraw. Someone got up quickly, held open the door and escorted her out with a delicate blending of tact and chivalry. It was Robert Cecil. This was coals of fire indeed.

Completely unnerved, and haunted by a curious guilt she could not analyse, Penelope cried all the way home in her coach.

So now the two most celebrated members of the Devereux family were imprisoned in different parts of London. Though Penelope's prison was very comfortable, and she was allowed to receive visitors. The Essex faction rallied round her; they thought she was a martyred heroine and persuaded her to feel like one — it was much pleasanter than that disagreeable sense of guilt which she soon managed to forget.

It was infuriating to be shut away at Stratford, unable to share in the conferences between Southampton, Danvers, Cuffe and Anthony Bacon, as they matured their plans for a concerted action with Charles and the Scottish Ambassadors if it came to an armed rising. Robin's position was desperate. On Maundy Thursday, after twenty-four weeks at the Lord Keeper's, he was taken to Essex House, but this was no release; all his own servants had been cleared out first, and he was still closely guarded, he might almost have been in the Tower.

Even Frank was only allowed to enter her home for a few hours every day. The one possible motive for this restriction was puerile and odious when applied to a husband and wife whose devotion had grown and deepened in their tribulation. In any case, the Queen's petty spite was soon made to look ridiculous. Dorothy Northumberland, coming down in May to see Penelope, announced that Frank was pregnant.

On the 5th June, 1600, eight months after his return from Ireland, Essex was brought to York House for an enquiry into his mismanagement of the war, before a Commission consisting of the

Archbishop, the Lord Treasurer, the Lord Chief Justice, four judges, and ten other peers and Officers of State, including Robert Cecil. This was not a formal trial, but Cecil was a devious worker, and if he had tampered with the evidence, the trial would follow. If, for instance, false proofs were forthcoming that Essex had been conspiring with the arch-enemy Tyrone, and aiming to make himself King.

Penelope waited at Stratford in a ferment of emotions. By tonight their secret messengers might be on the way to Scotland and Ireland. It would take over a week to organise a treason trial before the House of Lords; they had counted on that. By then, Charles could be in London, as well as the Scottish Ambassadors. What was happening now at York House might settle Charles's fate as well as Robin's — and if they were unlucky, that fate would be short, sharp and bloody. An axe on Tower Hill.

Penelope prowled up and down the gallery, physically affected by the strain, with fidgeting hands and a nervous cramp in her stomach. It was a showery day and the children, driven indoors, overflowed into every room. She almost wished there were not so many of them. Three months of house-arrest had sharpened her temper.

"What will they do to my uncle?" asked his namesake, the fifteen-year-old Essex Rich.

Penelope rounded on her. "Good grief, if I knew that, do you think I should be nearly mad from the suspense? I suppose you can't help being a fool. You can at least keep out of my sight. Or hold your tongue."

Essex turned white, her pretty face wavered and contorted. Her small half-sister Isabel studied her with an air of cool enquiry that made her ridiculously like Charles.

"You're too old to cry," she said judicially.

Essex gave a sort of choked bellow, and Penelope was contrite.

"My pet, I'm sorry. I didn't mean to be so unkind. There, love — don't take it to heart."

"Essex is a cry-baby," announced Isabel.

"Be quiet, you little toad!" snapped Penelope.

Her eldest son Robert had been lying

on the floor, reading. He jumped up and took charge of his half-sister.

"Come on, Bel. It's stopped raining. We'll go down to the pond and fish for newts."

Isabel was delighted to go anywhere with her particular hero. Robert was a handsome boy of thirteen with a lavish share of the Devereux charm and a remarkably placid disposition. Heaven knows where he gets that from, thought his distracted mother.

It was past ten o'clock, and she was leaning at her window in a stupor of exhausted hope and dread, when she heard the clop of a lone horseman on the Bow Road.

She ran down into the hall as the porter admitted Anthony Bagot, who had been Robin's friend and servant since they were boys together at Chartley.

"Tony — tell me quickly!"

"He was severely censured, madam, and sent home again, still a prisoner."

"And the charges?"

"Disobedience and contempt, based on his conduct of the war, and his returning to England without permission. His lordship owned his guilt, very humbly, and said that God had so afflicted his conscience, because he had defied the Queen, that nothing they did to him could add to his misery."

Poor Robin, she could hardly bear to think of the tormented heart-searching which must have led to that cry of remorse. Yet the news in itself was not too disastrous.

"There was no other indictment?" she asked Bagot. "Nothing of the kind we suspected?"

"Nothing, my lady. The entire time from eight in the morning till an hour ago was taken up with these lesser accusations. They kept him kneeling before them on the stone floor for two whole hours. Until the Archbishop procured him a cushion. And later, when he had stood so long he could scarce keep upright, His Grace insisted that he should have a stool. The others could not rest content with reciting his misdemeanours, over and over again. They wanted to glory in his disgrace."

Penelope closed her eyes and had a clear vision of Robin, every layer of protection brutally stripped away, losing all sense of what he was and had been, all consciousness of fame and achievement, as they broke him down to the level of a lonely penitent kneeling to confess his failures in a carefully-staged scene of public humiliation. I'll never forgive any of them for this, she thought.

"They went too far," said Tony. "For he behaved so well, bore it all with such patience and dignity that the spectators — there were about two hundred of them — were all drawn over to his side before the end. Many were in tears."

Tony was nearly in tears himself, and he looked worn out. Penelope led him into the parlour, sent for a flagon of wine, and made him drink while they talked.

"Who do you think was the chief prosecutor?" said Tony.

"Sir Edward Coke, I suppose, the Attorney-General."

"Oh, Coke blustered and bullied, as he always does. But the most cogent attack on his lordship came from the man who owes more to his generosity than anyone else in the kingdom."

"You can't mean Francis Bacon?"

"Indeed I do, madam. So busy telling us how it distressed him to accuse his former patron, and poisoning the air with every word he uttered. I could have killed the little rat with my bare hands."

Bacon's ingratitude must have hurt Robin more than anything — Robin, who had never deserted a friend in his life. Bacon's cousin, Robert Cecil, on the other hand, had apparently said very little and shown no personal animosity towards his fallen adversary. One thing was obvious, at any rate. Cecil had not laid a trail of false evidence. According to Charles's reckoning, that meant he was honest after all. There would be no need for an armed rising; she must be thankful for that. And as for Robin, the worst ordeal was over. An official censure did not impose any particular penalty; the Commissioners had said openly that they had never doubted his loyalty, and several of them had hinted that he might now expect some clemency from the Queen.

All the same, Penelope was disturbed by the ruthless way they had dealt with his actual mistakes in Ireland. Their attitude had hardened, and she could guess the reason. She asked Tony what he thought.

He hesitated, cupping his hands round his goblet, and frowning.

"I heard some of the onlookers say that he would have been judged more leniently five months ago. It did not then rank as a crime for a general to be worsted by the Irish. So many good men had come to grief that the mission seemed hopeless."

"Yes. It's strange that Essex's dearest friend should be the one to shatter that myth so inconveniently."

"I'm sure your brother does not see it in that light," said Tony swiftly. "No one could expect Lord Mountjoy to ruin his own reputation out of consideration for the Earl."

"But no one thought that Lord Mountjoy had a reputation worth ruining," retorted Penelope, with a trace of irony. "I wonder how we were all so blind."

For they had been fantastically wide of the mark, Robin as far out as anyone. All through Charles's steady climb at Court there had been a potential brilliance about him that was never quite fulfilled. He was the intelligent amateur, the detached observer, not entirely committed to any ambition or career — except, of course, to his passionate love for Penelope. Some wits had maliciously suggested that loving Penelope was Mountjoy's full-time occupation. They would not make that jibe again.

Once he had taken control in Ireland, his true vocation had emerged, the proper employment for the cool brain, the subtle strength, the reserves of untapped energy. And a very surprising vocation it was. The inexperienced and bookish Lord Mountjoy had turned out to be a born general, one of that rare breed of heaven-sent commanders who never put a foot wrong and snatch every fight into a victory.

Lying in bed that night, released from her immediate fears for Robin, Penelope thought about Charles instead, and went over all the details she had garnered from the various reports and letters that had filtered through from Ireland. When he got to Dublin, it had been rather what she had imagined:

the Army, sullen and demoralised, had resented Essex's successor, the well-dressed courtier who was so careful of his comfort. (The Earl had never noticed what he ate or drank.) The new Lord Deputy did not respond to the cocksure captains who plied him with good advice; his civil snubs were like a bucket of cold water. When he went into the field, his officers despised him for sleeping in his tent every afternoon — whoever heard of such supine lethargy in a man of thirty-six? It then transpired that his lordship was uncommonly active in the middle of the night, and liable to turn up wherever he was least expected, probably at some forward outpost where the guard was drunk or dozing. After a few embarrassing incidents of this kind, the regiments acquired a very healthy respect for their new master. As they began to fight under him, they made an exhilarating discovery; whenever the Lord Deputy manœuvred them round the little hills and rivers, he had some miraculous instinct which told him exactly where to place them. His plans worked out infallibly, and his long-defeated troops, after months of ignominious rout, actually found themselves hammering the Irish.

There were no pitched battles yet; Charles was feeling his way and nursing his men back to confidence in a campaign of small skirmishes. He had that humdrum but most necessary quality of all great soldiers: he refused to be tempted beyond his Army's capacity. He set about the rebel bands by hunting them out one at a time, worrying them into corners, like a sheepdog, tireless and tenacious. He had won the trust and then the affection of his troops, and there was a heartening conviction that between them they were going to win the war.

And she had never suspected that any of these things could happen. How obtuse she must have seemed to him, and how she must have hurt him by her lack of faith. For surely a man would be aware of his own potential genius, even when he had no opportunity to try it out? She remembered his frequent efforts to go off and fight overseas, and his disappointment when he had first been rejected for the Irish command, followed by that single outburst of pique in which he told her that Robin had no head for strategy. She did not quite believe this, even now, though she was ready to admit that Charles had turned out the better general of the two. It was a pity they had not been in Ireland together, they would have made a splendid partnership — and they might do so yet, she thought, her spirits reviving a little. For if the changed situation in Ireland had put Robin at a temporary disadvantage, it was certain that Charles's success would increase his importance and influence at home; he would be a far more valuable ally for Robin in the long run. She finally went to sleep feeling more cheerful than she had done for many months.

The next few weeks were an anti-climax. The findings of the Commission seemed to have no effect, one way or another, on that enigmatic old woman in the Palace. It was the end of July before she decided that the former Lord Deputy of Ireland had been sufficiently chastened. The favourite had a longer sentence to serve. He was set free, to live how and where he chose, with one embargo. He was forbidden to come to Court.

A few days later a Royal Messenger rode to Stratford with a similar message for Penelope.

4

PENELOPE did not mind being
exiled from the Court. There was
only one place she wanted to go,
the morning she was set free, and she
drove there immediately. Essex House
was crystallised in her memory as she
had known it for years: the hub of
fashionable London and the headquarters
of the foreign service, sumptuous rooms
and galleries crowded with courtiers and
suitors, soldiers and retainers. It was a
shock to see the hall nearly empty, a place
of chilly draughts and hollow echoes, like
a deserted stage at the end of a play.

Robin was writing in his study; he got
up to greet her and she ran forward and
clung to him, pressing her face against his
sleeve. Then she stood back and surveyed
him anxiously, dreading to see what they
had done to him.

She was agreeably surprised. Robin was
pale, as always, and far too thin, but his
eyes were steady and unshadowed, and

he carried himself with his old assurance, almost with a kind of sober gaiety.

"Well?" she enquired, tentative. "How is it with you, my very dear lord?"

"I'm a free man, exalting in my freedom — a pleasure I'd nearly forgotten."

"Yes, it's odious to be tied to one house, isn't it? We weren't bred for captivity, you and I."

"Oh, my poor Pen! You've suffered so much too, and all on my account. I am indeed sorry for it."

"You need not be; I brought my troubles on myself. What's more, I fear I did you more harm than good by my meddling."

"You meddled with great courage," he said, smiling. "And if you were indiscreet, it would ill become me, of all men, to tell you so. I've been an intractable subject, Pen. From now on, it will be different. I've had my lesson."

They sat by the window and talked. She was amazed at the calm way he discussed his fall. He was quite without bitterness.

"I was wrong to flout Her Majesty's orders," he said. "Now I can face my conscience and my countrymen and make a fresh start. A couple of months rusticating in the country, and then I'll come back here and await my summons to the Palace. She'll send for me soon. She'll forgive me and be kind to me, I know that. At heart she is all compassion. She has shown me such great favour in the past, and the bond between us is too strong for Cecil or Ralegh to sever. Dorothy says she talks of me continually; that augurs well."

Penelope was made a little uneasy by his trust in the Queen's ultimate goodness. Robin had never let life corrupt him, he had the innocence of the single eye. Blessed are the pure in heart — but perhaps the Beatitudes were not the most helpful guide to the complex mind and motives of Elizabeth Tudor. It would be tragic if she rejected him now. Still, their friends all agreed that she liked to hear Robin's name these days, and listened eagerly when his praises were sung. Behind the despot's harsh indifference, there still remained the woman's sick yearning after her fascinating cousin, and that would do as well as any more noble

214

impulse, if it got him back where he belonged.

Robin was seeing life in glowing colours this morning. He was so grateful to Frank; she had saved his life and then his sanity, no man ever had a more perfect companion.

"You have all been such incomparable friends," he said. "You and Doll and Harry — and Charles. I shan't forget the heroic plans he made to protect me." He hesitated. There must be a slight embarrassment in speaking of Charles, the unassuming lieutenant whose ability he had misjudged, and who was now scoring all the triumphs he had expected for himself. Robin made an effort. "The news from Ireland grows brighter every week. Charles is set to out-general us all. You must be very proud of him, my dear."

"Yes, I am," she said simply. "Though I should enjoy his success with a quieter mind, if it did not threaten to increase his peril. Tyrone has told off a hundred picked men to spy out for Charles and kill him."

"Tyrone never paid me that compliment," said Robin evenly. He added, with a quick sympathy, that she must not fret; none of the Irish could shoot straight.

She thought it would be tactful to change the subject, which she did by asking what Robin thought of another of his friends.

He was magnanimous, even towards Bacon. "Poor Francis, he was only acting professionally, as a lawyer employed by the Crown. There's no malice in him. He wrote me a long letter of explanation. Here, you can read it."

He rummaged in a leather box on the table, found the letter and gave it to her. Bacon's prose was plausible and seductive, and it revealed precisely nothing, except that the writer wanted to be on both sides at once. That, and a timid shrinking from a leader whose ambition frightened him. He likened Robin to Icarus in the fable, who had wings of wax which melted when he flew too near the sun, so that he fell into the sea and was drowned. Was that a fair analogy? Many people would say so. Shaking their heads wisely over his disasters, they missed the essential quality that Robin had in common with Icarus they had both soared valiantly into the heights from a world where most men plodded like peasants. And Robin was not drowning; unlike Icarus, he knew how to swim.

Henry Cuffe, his political secretary, came in with some query, and Penelope went upstairs to find her sister-in-law.

Frank greeted her eagerly.

"What do you make of Robin?"

"I can do nothing but marvel at him. Frank, I expected clouds of brooding and despair, and he is so serene. I had not believed it possible. This must be your doing. He speaks of you with such deep emotion, I'm sure your ears must be burning."

Frank flushed with pleasure. She was looking very handsome and contented, four months pregnant, and concentrating on the immediate pleasure of getting her husband away for a spell in the country. They would laze through the hours in a green garden and go on with the course of study they had begun while he was in prison; there were still so many books they wanted to read.

Penelope entered into her plans with a warm affection and wished them a happy holiday. But the summer would not last for ever.

"When you return," she said, "Robin seems certain that the Queen will send for him. Do you share his confidence?"

Frank drew in her lower lip, frowning a little. "I am sure she intends to reinstate him. Else why didn't she banish him to our estates in Wales or Staffordshire? Why let him loose a mile from her Court and all his powerful allies, here in London where he is a popular idol? She must mean to whistle him back when it pleases her. If only she doesn't wait too long."

"Too long?"

"Yes. Robin is so active and impetuous, he demands the same response in others. He hasn't the gift of patience, hardly thinks it a gift worth having. And the Queen is infinitely patient — an artist in delay. My father used to tell me she preferred that slow tempo, even when she was young. It's achieved her purpose many times, but it won't answer with Robin. If she keeps him dangling in suspense, she'll break his spirit, both hope and contrition may wear out before she is ready to forgive

218

him, and then I don't know which way he'll turn. Penelope, there are moments when I am so dreadfully afraid."

"It's no wonder." Penelope wanted to reassure her, without examining this depressing prophecy too closely. "You have been through such torments in the past year, and your condition makes you apprehensive. The Queen is an exasperating old woman, I hold no brief for her, but remember she knows the fine balance of Robin's temper as well as you or I. Since she still has an Earl Marshal, she'll put him to work rather than let him rot — you must admit she abominates waste."

Frank laughed, and said that Penelope was right; she must not let her fancies make a fool of her. Of course the Queen would calculate the exact moment to relent. She always had before.

They went down to join Robin, and found his secretary still with him, standing square in front of the chimney-piece and apparently making a speech. Henry Cuffe was four years older than his master, a celebrated Greek scholar and a former Oxford professor, who traded on the don's right to be eccentric. He prided himself on saying exactly what he thought, which was often uncomplimentary. Charles called him Honest Henry, a nickname with a sting. Robin had encouraged his forthright manner, having always allowed his principal servants to treat him more like an equal than a demi-god. Though he did not seem to be enjoying what Cuffe was saying this morning. He sat fidgeting with his pen, his expression decidedly strained.

"How your lordship can be so blind." The rather hectoring tone grated. "Can't you see how this apathy lessens your consequence? Pious resignation may do for some men, it's not what we expect from you, sir. You still hold four of the highest offices in the State. Very well, then. Insist on your claims to fulfil them."

"When you have finished, Cuffe," said Robin, "perhaps you will give place to Lady Essex."

Cuffe turned to the two women and bowed, quite unabashed. "Your ladyships will pardon my lack of ceremony, you know me for a man of plain words. Lady Rich, I invoke you as a most welcome ally. I was telling his lordship what a poor impression his present meekness is creating among the multitudes who follow him. You are a Devereux born, madam, and a fearless fighter — aren't you astounded at this strange docility from the head of your house?"

Penelope had been astounded, but she was not prepared for a string of unflattering comments from her brother's secretary. She glanced at Robin and saw that he was becoming annoyed. Cuffe took no notice of the danger signals.

"He was altogether too lowly before the Commissioners. Matters are come to a pretty pass when the Earl of Essex resorts to cringing abasement . . . "

"I do not cringe!" Robin brought his hand down on the table with a crack that made them all jump. "And I will not tolerate your damnable insolence. You'll learn who rules here, Cuffe, and you'll not trespass on my docility again."

He was furiously angry, but with none of the hysterical overtones of his rages against the Queen. There was instead

221

a stern austerity which his wife and sister had not encountered before. Cuffe remembered it from the ramparts of Cadiz, the quarter-deck of *Due Repulse*. Having gone too far, he began a hasty recantation.

"I meant no disrespect to your lordship, my zeal ran away with me. I was speaking for your own good, and if I have been overbold, my lord, I am assured you are too generous to hold it against me."

Robin ignored him, reached for a small gold bell, and rang it. His page appeared in the doorway.

"Fetch my steward."

The boy withdrew. Robin sat staring into space, his profile stony and impersonal, in a silence none of the others dared to break. Cuffe tugged at his beard, they could hear his heavy breathing.

When Sir Gelly Meyrick came in, Robin said to him, "Mr. Cuffe is leaving my service. You will see that he is paid what I owe him. He is not to be admitted to this house, on any pretext whatever."

The steward was thunderstruck. He gaped from one man to the other.

"My lord!" Cuffe's appeal was desperate. "I beseech you, don't turn me off. Give me one further chance, and I promise I'll not offend you again. You know I would rather die than leave your lordship." He was genuinely devoted to Essex, and almost in tears.

The steward took his part. "I don't know the cause of your displeasure, my lord, but surely Mr. Cuffe's long years of loyalty have earned him some consideration . . . "

"I gave you an order, Meyrick." Robin's voice was deadly. "You will see that it is carried out."

"Yes, my lord."

Meyrick knew better than to argue. He took the unhappy Cuffe away with him.

Robin remained perfectly still. The earlier mood of serenity had been driven out, but this was the other side of the same medal: an absolute and rigid self-command. He spoke to his wife with an unusual formality.

"I regret that your ladyship had to witness that unedifying scene."

"My dear," Frank crossed the room to him. "Cuffe was outrageous; I have always thought him ill-bred and a trouble-maker. And yet, a summary dismissal — was

223

that a little unjust? You've accorded him the privilege of lecturing you like an undergraduate, you can't entirely blame him for his presumption."

"I could overlook presumption in any other matter, but not in this. Don't you know what he was after, Frank? Goading me, inciting me to challenge the Queen's authority by some open act of self-assertion. That's the dangerous path which leads to sedition."

Frank made a small movement of fear. He took her hand and held it against his cheek.

"I can't afford the finer shades of justice," he said, "while I'm fighting for my salvation. After all these months of anguish, beating down the devil in my own soul, do you think I'm going to risk an assault from the same enemy, when he comes to me in another guise?"

It was not until then that Penelope fully realised the inner stress that Robin had endured in the conflict between his duty as a subject and his natural pride. Virtue had won a costly and precarious victory. She hoped the Queen would have the grace to reward it.

Part Four

Traitors' Gate

October 1600 – March 1601

1

THE high hopes of the summer dwindled away in frustration.

Penelope, who had been down at Leez nursing Rich through a trying illness, came back to Essex House in mid-October and found an oppressive darkening of the horizon. There was still no message from the Palace. The endless strain was having a lacerating effect on Robin's state of mind: what he craved for now was constant mental stimulus, so it was lucky that his friends were rallying round him. His house had again become the centre of a faction. One of the first people Penelope met was Henry Cuffe, hurrying importantly with a sheaf of papers under his arm.

"I see you've relented towards Honest Henry," she said later, when she was alone with her brother.

"Southampton persuaded me. And Meyrick says he knows too many of my secrets. Besides," Robin gave her a deprecating glance, "he came and pleaded his cause so piteously. He said that I must surely understand the miseries of a disgraced servant who begs in vain to be forgiven. You can imagine how that thrust went home. What could I do but give him back his office?"

There was nothing else he could do, being Robin. He could not withhold his generosity in order to punish Cuffe. Neither could he make out why anyone else should use these methods towards himself. The Queen's hostility baffled and hurt him more every day; his confidence was ebbing, and with it his patient humility. Frank had been right: the Queen's delaying tactics were the most disastrous treatment for anyone who surrendered himself so entirely to the present.

There was a new anxiety looming, a topic that slid into every discussion of his prospects. The farm of sweet wines.

This was a monopoly that the Queen had granted him in 1592, the right to levy a tax on every cask of wine that was imported from the Continent. It formed virtually the whole of his income, and the patent was due to expire. Robin's future rested on whether the Queen would renew it. Of course he implored her to do so, but it was an extremely unfortunate moment to have to write to her about money, because all those pages of unswerving devotion which he sent her every day had begun to read like professional begging letters.

At the end of October the blow fell. The farm of sweet wines was to revert to the Crown. Financially, Essex was ruined. The Devereux estates had always been encumbered, and he had been living for years on this one vast monopoly. Living as a public benefactor, furnishing ships and raising regiments, keeping the Government supplied with foreign intelligence, showering patronage on poets and scholars, besides helping a legion of other dependents and maintaining a ceremonial state fit for the most illustrious Englishman of his day. In spite of his enormous revenue, he had run up an alarming series of debts. Now the monopoly was gone, and his creditors, seeing that the Queen had withdrawn her support, would soon descend on him like vultures. He would be driven out of the field of national affairs as brutally as if she had actually banished him. No one could be less useful to his country than a nobleman without any money.

"So now we know what her fine promises are worth," he said bitterly.

Frank, determined to be fair, suggested that the Queen might not appreciate his difficulties. "Princes don't have to shift and contrive as we do."

"Why deceive yourself, my dear? She's let those villains corrupt her; she's weak, perfidious — I always said no woman was meant to rule a kingdom, and now she's given hers into the hands of Mr. Secretary Macchiavelli. With Ralegh and Cobham to abet him."

He had a prophetic sense of doom. He had lost the advantage of managing the Queen and he had been superseded by a crew of godless mercenaries who had sold the reversion of the Crown to the Spanish claimant. There was no absolutely certain evidence against Cecil and his cronies, but any number of hair-raising rumours, half-proofs and deductions came pouring into Essex House, to be sifted and collated by Henry Cuffe, who had stepped into Anthony Bacon's shoes. Anthony had not deserted his patron; he was a complete invalid now, living in his brother's house at Twickenham. In the absence of the Bacons and Mountjoy, Cuffe was by far the most capable of the select inner ring surrounding Essex. The others were Southampton, Penelope, Charles Danvers, Gelly Meyrick and Christopher Blount, who had been sent down from Staffordshire by his wife to do what he could for her son. The gentle and self-effacing Frances kept in the background, awaiting the birth of her baby.

There was only one chance of saving the situation: Essex must somehow achieve a meeting with the Queen. Their friends at Court were convinced that she still hankered after her former favourite, and if only he could spend an hour alone with her, surely his charm would win the day. He had always been able to twist her round his little finger.

Since the Queen's intolerable defects of pride, conceit and contrariness would not let her admit her need for a man she really loved, they would have to find another way of manoeuvring him back into her orbit. The most obvious move was to excite public sympathy. His bankers were waiting on events, which was encouraging; he would have a few months' grace before the creditors closed in. His friends must work night and day to rouse support for the champion of a free England. With all the main sections of the community solidly behind him, he could demand a Privy Councillor's undoubted right of access to his Sovereign. What exactly they meant by the crucial word demand was something they were beginning to discuss in confidential whispers. Subjects did not demand their rights from Queen Elizabeth. But as the movement gained impetus, and the number of supporters rose rapidly, so the whispers grew louder.

They soon had four Earls among their allies. Southampton and Rutland, of course; Rutland was Essex's particular protégé, the boy whom he had married to his stepdaughter, Elizabeth Sidney. There were also Bedford and Sussex, as well as Lord Cromwell, Lord Mounteagle, Lord Sandys, and a host of knights, including a cousin of Ralegh's and several of the Percies. And there was great enthusiasm in the City.

Penelope had never worked so hard in her life, holding court as her brother's political hostess, driving out in her coach to hunt up possible adherents, arguing and persuading, coaxing the laggards. She was thriving on the excitement, and Essex House teemed with people and plans.

"It's like old times," she said, sweeping through the gallery in a gorgeously-encrusted golden dress and the widest of farthingales.

It was not like old times, as she would have seen if she had ever let her energies run down, and taken a dispassionate look at what was happening. Perhaps she did not want to see too clearly; there was a slackening of principle, a tough, irreverent cynicism about ways and means, which the young Penelope — and the young Essex — would once have found completely alien. And in spite of the distinguished group at the core, too many of the gentlemen who swaggered or loitered in the great rooms, devouring endless meals, were hardly more than adventurers: rakes and gamblers, as well as malcontents of every description. Catholics and Puritans rubbed shoulders with men who never used God's name except in blasphemy. Essex's Utopian dreams of religious freedom had brought him some strange associates; he did not seem to mind, and had redressed the balance by filling the place with clergy. He had always collected parsons, and he needed these black-robed zealots to give him their blessing and remove any sense of guilt from the hatred that was corroding his spirit.

For he really hated his adversaries now, not Cecil and Ralegh only, but the Queen. Old resentments were recalled and exaggerated; the happy memories turned sour. He knew he could still captivate her, given the chance, but that merely made him despise her. The whole history of their relationship filled him with disgust and contempt. Belphoebe had been transformed into Jezebel.

In fact, he himself was becoming a major problem to his own side. Christmas passed, Frank's daughter was born, supporters flocked to the great house on the Thames, and it was said that the Queen and her Secretary were thoroughly frightened of the national hero. The faction were jubilant. They had come to realise that it would be a waste of time for Essex merely to force a meeting with the Queen; he would have to remove the traitors and dominate the Council. He was certainly strong enough. But Essex kept lapsing into periods of sullen brooding, and refused to make any definite decisions. In his sociable phases he was liable to break into violent invective against the Queen, often in front of the very last people who ought to hear it. Honest as ever, he was not cut out for conspiracy.

There was a morning when he had several visitors from the Court, moderate men not yet committed to his party, among them Sir John Harrington, the Queen's godson. Essex was complaining about his prolonged exile. The Queen, he said, was playing a game of cat-and-mouse with him. She would never recall him of her own accord. Harrington disagreed. Let his lordship be patient, she would have him back in all his glory sooner or later.

"Though I won't foretell the date," added Harrington. "No one can predict exactly what course she will follow."

"Save that it won't be a straight one," retorted Robin. "The old woman's courses are as crooked as her carcass."

There was an incredulous silence, while the visitors wondered if they had heard him correctly. Robin left them in no doubt; he stalked restlessly up and down the room, enlarging on his theme. Kit Blount laughed nervously. Penelope saw the bewilderment in Elizabeth Rutland's eyes; she gazed at her stepfather as though she could hardly recognise the same man who had brought her up so carefully, and moulded her young husband to the most flawless pattern of chivalry. Jack Harrington was plainly horrified. He made his escape as soon as he could, almost dragging Penelope with him.

"I couldn't stay and listen a second longer," he exploded, as soon as the door was shut. "What demon possesses him? He must be ill."

"He's been treated abominably, you

know that, and he never could guard his tongue. Do you expect him to put on a mantle of hypocrisy?" Penelope was privately cursing Robin's indiscretion.

"I expect the Earl Marshal to employ the language of loyalty and respect," said Harrington bleakly. "And the manners of a gentleman. To fling such personal insults at any woman, let alone his Sovereign — it appals me to hear him sink so low. While his satellites do nothing but fawn round him, to applaud or condone. Lady Rich, you must know what evils encompass you here. You ought to break away and go home as soon as you can."

It was Penelope's turn to look incredulous.

"I notice Rich keeps his distance," persisted Harrington. "Well, you may not set much store by his example, but there's one man whose good opinion you do care for. What do you suppose Lord Mountjoy would have said to that filthy jibe? What would he say if he could see you in the company that frequents your brother now? This house is little better than a tavern for cut-throats. As for the Earl, it might in charity be claimed that his troubles have affected his wits. I can hardly believe him sane.

Penelope lost her temper. "Be damned to you, Jack — who gave you leave to preach at me, or call my brother a madman? If you don't like our manner of talking, you have your remedy. Run back to your godmother, you impudent popinjay — we've no use for croakers and time-servers here."

Harrington bowed very stiffly and said he was sorry to have offended her, he had meant it for the best. As he took himself off, he remarked, "I shan't carry tales to Her Majesty. But make no mistake, the others will."

Penelope leant on the carved banister and watched him go. Foreshortened from above, she saw his dapper figure cross the hall and disappear into the London street. They had been fond of Jack — yes, and he had been overjoyed to kneel before Robin and receive from him the accolade of knighthood. Ungrateful little cur, she said aloud. She knew she was being unjust; just as she knew that coarse and brutal comment was a deviation from Robin's exacting standards of behaviour, but she had to smother her critical judgment and blame Harrington, because there had been several kind friends lately, trying to come between her and Robin. Didn't the fools realise that a man's sister could never desert him, no matter what he did? When you worked it out, that tie was the closest of all, with a special quality that rivalled all others. The shared childhood, the shared ancestry. There was no impulse, good or bad, in Robin's bloodstream that was not potentially present in hers also. For all the separateness of two distinct individuals, Penelope and Robin had felt an invisible force uniting them, right from the start, before she could read or he could speak.

As for those interfering outsiders, she knew how to deal with their impertinence.

A servant approached her. "Lord Dunkellin is asking for your ladyship."

She turned quickly. "Where is he? When did he arrive?"

This was the one thing that could distract her, for it always meant news from Charles. Richard de Bourgh, Lord Dunkellin, was the Earl of Clanrickarde's heir, a trusted officer under the successive

Lords Deputy; as a scion of the Irish aristocracy, it was easy for him to travel between the two kingdoms, and any letter he brought her was uncensored. He was waiting in her apartments, a tall and lively young man with russet colouring and fine Norman features.

She held out her hands to him; he kissed them both.

"Faith now, and it's glad I am to see your ladyship. I thought you'd have a welcome for your Mercury."

"Faith now, you were right." Laughing, she echoed the Irish lilt that Cambridge had not bred out of him. "How did you leave my dear lord? Tell me everything."

"He's in great heart, madam, and a paragon among warriors. Campaigning through the winter, as you know, which is unheard of. My rebel countrymen are highly indignant, they say it's no way for a nobleman to be acting. And there's his lordship harrying them six days a week, ten hours a day in the saddle. No winter quarters for him, nor soft lying in castles either, but a truckle bed in a turf cabin — sure, you never saw the like of it."

Charles in a turf hut? No, she had never seen the like of it.

"He's in good health?"

"Don't you be fretting; he wraps up warm and drinks buttermilk by the quart, and sees to it that he's well served, even in a bog. His dinner must be hot, and his armour bright as the noonday, or he'll know the reason — without ever raising his voice. He's as cordial and modest as you please, living out beside his troops, and we love him for it, but by the Saints, we don't forget who is our commander."

Penelope was entranced by the glimpse of Charles with his army. He was in his element, she had accepted this new side of him, and there was a brave, clean simplicity about it, refreshing in a world of intrigue. She clasped the packet that Dunkellin had given her, it was addressed to the Honourable Lady Rich in Charles's beautiful italic hand. Dunkellin said tactfully that he ought to pay his respects to Lord and Lady Essex.

When he had gone, Penelope slit the seals of her letter and settled down to enjoy it. The result was unexpected and sobering. Charles's devotion was as satisfactory as ever, and he described his daily adventures, and the turf cabin, with the laconic wit she knew so well, but his main object was quite different. He had been getting very disturbing reports from London, all the more disturbing because he could not make out what Essex was trying to do. He did not ask Penelope to abandon her brother's cause, but he warned her not to get involved in any unlawful bid for power. Charles no longer believed that Cecil was in league with the Spaniards. (She knew this already, for he had emphasised it in a message to Southampton some time ago.) Therefore, if Essex made any attempt to defy or coerce the Queen, he would be guilty of treason without any moral justification. Charles said he was sorry to disagree with Penelope's opinion of Cecil, whose character was the real point at issue, but he was writing as her husband when he asked her to suspend her own judgment and submit to his authority on a matter of such vital importance. He reminded her, very gently, that it was her duty to do as he told her. She should ignore the fables of a Spanish plot, temper her devotion to Essex with common sense, and resist every scheme which had the faintest flavour of sedition. All this was conveyed with the greatest affection and restraint, but the underlying attitude was decidedly austere.

Penelope read the letter through again, frowning at the close-packed lines until they ran together in a blur. She did not at all enjoy getting orders from Charles. She had grown used to her curious, independent status, and saw no reason why anyone should direct her actions, especially where they related to her own family.

He was assuming the rights of a husband, but was she in fact his wife? She had never been sure. She honestly believed that their boy-and-girl betrothal was still binding. This meant that her subsequent marriage to Rich was invalid; as long as Charles lived, she could never belong to any other man. But whether they were actually married — that was another story. She had never fully understood Charles's theological arguments about the sacred nature of a marriage by consent; she had a profound respect for the traditional forms and an elementary Catholicism, deep in her mind like an underground spring, which made her feel that you could not be properly married except in church. Her convictions had wavered backwards and forwards over the years. She was thirty-seven years old, the mother of nine children, and at the moment it appeared to her that she had never been married to anyone. It was a wry conclusion.

Yet the inference was plain. If Charles was not her husband, he had no claim on her obedience. The person she ought to obey was Robin, the head of her house, and her feudal overlord, who was also her true protector in a way that Charles had never been. It was Robin, not Charles, who had saved her from the scandal that nearly engulfed her after the birth of her first illegitimate child, and she was not going to desert him in his hour of need. She loved Charles dearly, and dreaded hurting him; at the same time she was irritated by his dogmatic pronouncements. How could he pretend, stuck there in his bog, to interpret Cecil's motives more accurately than the rest of them? She was having a series of annoyances, first from Jack Harrington, and now from Charles, and the climax came that evening with a deputation urging her to tackle Robin, who had slipped into one of his moods of hopeless depression.

Southampton, Cuffe and Kit Blount had been trying unsuccessfully to brace him.

"But we might as well have talked to a graven image," said her stepfather. "You must go and put some fight into him, Pen. Frank's too meek and cautious. You're the one he needs."

"Can't we leave him tonight? He may sleep it off."

"He won't," objected Cuffe. "Consider the effect these withdrawals are having on our well-wishers. It's plain that the Earl's fortunes will never improve unless he is prepared to enter the Palace, lay hold of his enemies, and present himself as the Queen's chief Minister in conditions that brook no refusal. There are hundreds of us ready to ensure his success, straining at the leash to go, and what does his lordship do? Shuts himself up like a hermit and won't answer when we speak to him. Some of our fellows are beginning to murmur, they say he hasn't the stomach for such an enterprise." Penelope tried to interrupt; Cuffe's rather hard voice went on. "I'm not among them, madam. We three here, Lord Southampton and Sir Christopher and I, have seen Lord Essex lead his men into action, we know the true quality of his spirit, yet how can we convince others when he gives us so little help? If your ladyship could reason with him, he might pay attention to you."

Penelope could not refuse such an appeal. She found Robin sitting in a deliberate atmosphere of gloom, with only one light burning. He was doing nothing, gazing at nothing, his elbows propped on his knees; the eloquent line of his head and shoulders slouched in despair.

She said briskly that there was no sense in sitting in the dark, took a taper and lit the rest of the candles. The glowing pageant of the Flemish tapestries sprang into brightness around them.

"That's more lively," she said. "Did you see Dunkellin? I expect he had a letter for you also."

It had crossed her mind that a homily from Charles might have set off this particular mood.

Robin condescended to answer. "I suppose you can guess the gist of that letter. Mountjoy won't bring over the Irish army."

"You'd heard that already. He told Southampton weeks ago."

Robin muttered that his oldest friend had deserted him. The words were seeping with self-pity.

"No such thing," said Penelope. "It happens that Mountjoy doesn't share our mistrust of Cecil, so he sees no immediate cause for action, and however wrong he may be, he's entitled to judge for himself. What's more, he has his duty as Lord Deputy: we none of us want him to leave his work unfinished. There's no question of desertion, Robin. His loyalty to you remains unchanged."

Robin laughed. It was not an agreeable sound. "So Brutus is an honourable man? Well, you may put the best gloss you can on your lover. Any simpleton can understand the Lord Deputy's new scruples. Since he's gone hunting after glory on his own account he needn't trouble to keep faith with those who can no longer advance him. I was worth cultivating once; now I'm likely to prove an embarrassment to his lordship. That's the way of the world; there's no profit in gratitude."

She stared at him, astounded and then furious. For the second time that day she let the frayed edge of her temper rip.

"How can you be so vile, to speak like that of Charles, after all the sacrifices he offered to make for you, all your years of friendship? Can't you bear the sting of those victories you should have won yourself? I thought your lordship had too noble a mind to be jealous."

The more she thought about it, the more angry she felt. She had resisted all attempts to undermine her allegiance to Robin. They had not touched her essential belief in his destiny and his righteous cause. It had remained for him to shake that belief by his sick suspicions and grievances. Was it for this that she was prepared to oppose Charles, rejecting the authority he had claimed after years of deep and unselfish love — so that she could hear him slandered by the leader they had both followed so faithfully?

"Who are you to cast stones at Mountjoy?" she blazed, her black eyes stormy. "Isn't it better to hunt after glory than to wallow in defeat? Whining because he won't bring you an army — good heavens, you don't need his army to get you into the Palace The case is altered since last year: you are a free man, with hundreds of followers in your retinue, and thousands of secret friends willing to declare for you in the City. Whether you should force your way to the Queen and put yourself at the head of her Government, that's for you alone to decide and you can't shift the burden. No one is asking you to act against your conscience. If you doubt Cecil's guilt or the nation's peril, then you can dismiss your minions and send them home. But if you see yourself as the saviour of Protestant England, then, for pity's sake, Essex, what are you waiting for? Do you need Charles Blount for your wet-nurse? We all know he's surpassed your efforts in the war with Tyrone; surely you are able to take a company of halberdiers as far as Whitehall, to look for one old woman? Or is that feat of daring beyond your powers? You know what your friends are whispering, while you sit here and mope? They are beginning to say that you've lost your valour."

That last sally did the trick, shocked him back into contact with reality. He straightened, flushing through his pallor.

"Who says that?" he demanded.

She shrugged. "I don't gossip with your detractors. Let Cuffe supply a list, it will increase your load of injuries."

"I don't need their names," he said slowly, "since I know the one that hurts most. That you should call me a coward, Penelope. I must indeed have cut a sorry figure, to merit that reproach."

This was authentic; a sharp and genuine distress. The imagined wrongs and the petulance vanished as he struggled free from his trance. She could tell that he was honestly trying to examine her accusation, the ugliest and most unnatural charge that a man of his temperament could face, flung at him by the beloved sister whose admiration had always been so precious. He glanced at her once, with a sort of entreaty, and then quickly away, biting his lip, utterly bereft.

Penelope was invaded by a terrible remorse.

"I didn't call you a coward," she said urgently. "I never meant — it was a snatch of ignorant malice that I should not have repeated. My unruly tongue got the better of me. Dear Robin, forgive me."

She held out her hand to him. He hesitated, not, she thought, resentfully, but because he was pathetically uncertain of her. Then he saw that she was entirely sincere. He took her hand, grasping it so tightly that he bruised the knuckles. They neither of them spoke; the right words were too hard to find.

His fingers were icy cold, she could feel him shivering.

"Does your head ache?" she asked, in quite another manner, to which he was well accustomed. He had heard that feminine concern so often, from his mother and sisters, his wife, his mistresses and his Queen.

He admitted that his head was aching a little.

"Why didn't you tell me?" Having released her pent-up feelings, Penelope was eager to find a rational cause for Robin's mysterious fits of melancholy. He had probably been ill for weeks; that would account for everything. "Why didn't you say, instead of making a martyr of yourself while I abused you? Lean back against the cushion, and I'll try to soothe away the pain. You ought to be in bed. What fools men are."

"And what shrews they have for sisters," murmured Robin with the shadow of a smile, as he lay back.

How odd a familiar face looked from above, like a map turned upside-down. With the closed eyes and the long curve of the eyelashes, he seemed strangely innocent, this delicate, over-wrought young man who had always driven himself to breaking point. Even in this passive state, he radiated a more than physical beauty — no wonder so many people had fallen under his spell. Whatever he became in the end, he had lit a fire in more hearts than any man for generations. England's darling; didn't that name belong among the prophecies about King Arthur? There was something Arthurian here; poetry and passion, distant trumpets sounding for a dedicated patriot, who lighted the dreams of ordinary mortals with a vision of high adventure, of life as it ought to be.

The quiet peace had its healing effect, while she flexed and lifted the fabric of his skin where it joined the tawny-brown hair, raising the pressure from inflamed veins, slipping the knot of muscular contraction. The intimate closeness of touch revived her sense of their affinity.

Some of her mental pictures must have passed through to him, for he said, "You always used to take care of me, Pen, do you remember? When we were children at Chartley, when my father was alive — how happy I was then." He sighed. "And after I came down from Cambridge, when Walter and I were in Wales. Hunting all day, and talking half the night, as boys do, reading Latin and Greek for pleasure; there was nothing I wanted then that I couldn't get by the hard exercise of my body or my brain. I was perfectly content, yet the sad thing is I couldn't go back. I should find nothing there except monotony."

"There are flaming swords," she said, "outside all our first Edens."

"Yes. And consolations. A Promised Land for those who have the vigour to reach it. I've been too long in the wilderness . . . They say I'm ambitious; it's not true. I haven't perverted power for my private advantage, or tyrannised over the weak. I don't care a fig for the trappings of luxury. God knows I don't aim for the Crown. All I ever asked was to serve my country. To live and die for England. If this is denied me, I'm like a dead man already." After a pause, he added, with a seeming inconsequence, "I'm certain that little hunchback is a traitor. He must be."

Penelope was thankful to hear the expressive warmth come back into his voice. She asked if his headache was better.

"It's almost gone, you've charmed away the pain. I shall recommend you as a white witch." Robin opened his eyes, stretched and sat up. "I'll write to King James in the morning. I should like to have the Scottish Ambassadors with me when I demand an audience of Her

Majesty. Then it will be plain to everyone that I come as a herald of her lawful heir, and not as an usurper. And Dunkellin can carry a message to Mountjoy; he may join us or not as he chooses. As you say, his presence is no longer vital to our enterprise."

"Robin." A new thought struck her. "If Charles stays away, you won't hold it against him later?"

Dominating the Queen and Council, with the whole country behind him, Essex would be able to mete out a deadly retribution to anyone who had displeased him.

But he seemed astonished by the question. "Why, what do you think I shall do, clap him in the Tower? He's far too valuable to the State and to me also. Yes, I dare say I called him a villain; we've both said things tonight that we regret. Whatever our differences, Charles is like my own brother. And you love him. My dearest Pen, you know very well that I could never do the smallest harm to either of you."

2

THE period of waiting for the Scottish Ambassadors was difficult for Robin, but Penelope now knew how to deal with symptoms of undue depression. She had only to remind him what was required from the victor of Cadiz.

On the 7th February, a new crisis broke. The Privy Council sent to know why the Earl was making such warlike preparations; he was ordered to appear before them and explain himself.

It was a Saturday, some of the brighter spirits had been to the Globe Theatre and paid for a special revival of an old play by Shakespeare, *Richard II*. In the public mind, that weak and effeminate monarch resembled the Queen in her dotage. And he was deposed by a popular hero, the cousin he had wronged.

Harry Southampton and Kit Blount were in the withdrawing-room, telling the ladies how they had packed the theatre and cheered the play, when Robin came in with the Council's message.

There was an immediate silence.

"Further," said Robin, "I've had an anonymous letter warning me not to go, and another to say that Ralegh and Cobham are going to murder me in my bed."

"Let them try!" Young Rutland moved closer to his wife's step-father, fiercely protective. "They'll have to cross a hedge of steel and a river of blood to do it. We can take care of your lordship."

"I've no doubt you can, Roger. But I don't lie down as a passive target for any man's villainy. Nor trot off meekly to the Council so that they can put me back in prison. These threats are intolerable."

"If you don't obey the Council," commented Kit, "they'll arrest you for contempt."

"Yes. So there's only one answer. We must go ahead without waiting for the Scottish envoys. Tomorrow I'll put my fortune to the test."

There was a tremor of excitement in his voice. Penelope thought he was tasting the moment of triumph when he would come glittering into the Queen's presence, the great statesman and warrior whom she had tormented and humiliated for sixteen long months. He would not let anyone hurt her; she would be treated with chivalry and deference, because she was a woman and her royal blood was sacred. His resentful anger would very likely vanish once he had her in his power; he had always been the gentlest of conquerors. But his most respectful petitions would in fact be commands, and they would both know it; that would be the subtle sweetness of his revenge.

Essex House was like a military camp. All that night there were comings and goings, lights in every room, the tread of hooted feet and the clatter of arms. Notes were sent out to summon all their friends. The leaders held a council of war.

Two things had to be done. They must enter the Palace and overcome the Guard so that they could seize the traitors and secure the custody of the Queen. They must also muster their supporters in the City. Essex had been promised a thousand men without delay, there would be plenty more to follow, and whoever held London held England.

Southampton was for marching straight to the Court; he thought the advantage of a surprise attack outweighed the extra troops they would collect in the City. Some of the older officers wanted to make sure of the City and then go in force to the Palace. There was a rather acrimonious discussion. Essex listened carefully to both parties, without giving his verdict. In the morning they still did not know what he had decided.

Penelope had snatched a couple of hours on her bed. She woke, feeling as fresh as a bird, to find the miniature army overflowing the forecourt into the hall: Robin's liveried servants, his patriotic friends, even the adventurers, with their lean, piratical faces, were an encouraging sight today. More people kept arriving. Old Lord Sandys was here; where was Bedford? Penelope, bubbling with energy, volunteered to go and fetch him.

Lord Bedford was in his own house, hearing a sermon; she had forgotten it was Sunday. He did not seem particularly anxious to come, but was quite unable to withstand the fiery beauty who carried him off in her chariot like a mythical goddess.

When they reached Essex House, there was some kind of commotion in the forecourt. Penelope left the coach and pushed her way in, craning to see over the massed block of backs. Everyone was shouting.

"What's happening?" she asked one of the young captains.

"It's a deputation from the Council, madam, trying to blandish the Earl with fair words. The Keeper and the Lord Chief Justice, with Worcester and your ladyship's uncle, Sir William Knollys. I'll clear a path for you. Hey, fellow! Make way for Lady Rich."

As they let her pass through, Penelope saw the deputation on the steps outside the great door. Worcester and her uncle looked reluctant and uncomfortable; the Lord Chief Justice was on the point of losing his temper. Their spokesman was Sir Thomas Egerton, Lord Keeper of the Great Seal of England, and Robin's former gaoler. He had a servant with him, bearing the Great Seal, which gave the visit an official solemnity. Or should have done. Robin, lounging against a stone pillar, was unimpressed; Kit and the others frankly pugnacious.

"There's a plot to take my life," Robin was saying. "Am I not justified in defending myself? Since it's plain I shall get no redress from any of you, for all your quoting of the law."

"My lord, you know that your complaints will receive an impartial hearing when you come before the Council . . . "

His words were battered down by the shouts from the forecourt. "Pay no heed, my lord . . . They undo you! They betray you!"

"This is outrageous," cried the Lord Keeper. He had taken off his hat, out of courtesy to Essex; now he put it on, a sign that he was speaking as the Queen's representative, and addressed the gathering in a loud voice. "I command you all, on your allegiance, to lay down your weapons and depart, which you ought all to do . . . "

"All! All! All!" chanted the crowd, swinging to the rhythm of their mockery.

Penelope had now reached the steps.

Through the tumult of hoots and jeers she heard the Lord Keeper say, "If you can't call your wolves to order, at least you can speak with us privately."

Robin surveyed his wolves. Arms linked, they pressed nearer, alert with malice and derision.

"It should interest you to learn that I have still these few friends who feel for my wrongs. However, I dare say your lordships would be happier indoors."

He ushered them into the house with a fine, formal grace. Someone called after him, "Kill them off and have done with it!" and there was a burst of laughter.

Deprived of their show, the men in the forecourt got bored, and began to shuffle and murmur, wondering how much longer his lordship would waste his time and their patience. The senior officers were having an excited argument among themselves. Penelope decided to investigate.

She went into the hall, to meet Robin returning alone, with a key in his hand.

"Robin — what have you done with them?"

"Locked them in my study." It sounded

like a schoolboy's prank, and he must have thought so too, for the disarming smile he gave her took her straight back into their childhood. "Well, what else could I do? They were so damnably inopportune. Where's Davies?"

"Here, my lord." A gentleman stepped forward from the group round the entrance.

Robin handed him the key. "Sir John, you must play warder to four very august prisoners. Use them with every civility, but for God's sake see they don't escape. I'm leaving you here, and Sir Gelly Meyrick, with my greatest treasures, my wife and family, in your charge, while I go to settle the score with my enemies."

He tweaked the brim of his high, plumed beaver to a martial tilt, and signalled to his page, Hal Tracy, who brought his cloak and gloves. Robin let the cloak furl back; the scarlet lining set off his magnificently broad shoulders and his impressive height. Then he went out on to the steps and drew his sword.

His myrmidons, gazing up at him, took in the meaning of the naked blade; they greeted him with a rapturous cheer.

Penelope had not heard anything like it since the glorious days after Cadiz. Her pulses throbbed with a loving pride which cast out fear. For an instant the radiance of all that enthusiasm was visible in her brother's face, like sunlight mirrored in clear water. The ranks in the forecourt divided to let him take the lead. Robin set forward with his easy, loping stride; the page at his heels was almost dancing with delight. Southampton and Kit Blount fell in at either side, a respectful pace behind their general, then Rutland and the other lords, Cuffe and Danvers ... The main body, about three hundred, too eager to keep step, jostled after them through the gate, crying exultantly, "To the Court! To the Court!"

But in the Strand Essex turned eastwards.

"That's mighty odd," remarked one of the guard who had been left behind. "He's going first to the City. I made sure he'd be hot-foot for Whitehall."

Penelope had thought so too. He must know that a surprise manoeuvre was likely to cause less bloodshed than a conventional attack by a large force whose coming was expected. News of the insurrection in the City would certainly get to the Palace ahead of them. Penelope thought Robin had made a tactical mistake. A stranger might have imagined that he was putting off his crucial encounter with the Queen. As though — it was ridiculous — as though, in his secret heart, he dreaded the moment when Elizabeth Tudor would see him as a rebel. Which is nonsense, Penelope told herself firmly; he's not afraid of the old termagant, he never was. Bewitched, at one time, yes. All those years when he had been the pupil, the faithful servant, the dear companion. But that was dust and ashes now. There was no point in hunting for imaginary difficulties, just because Robin's life was in danger, as it was bound to be, until this business was safely settled.

All the same, a curious flatness had clamped down on the day, on the empty Sunday silence and the nearly empty house. Penelope prowled about, feeling irritable. Presently she went up to the withdrawing-room where Frank was reading her Bible. The strain which made

Penelope so restless froze her sister-in-law into a static calm.

Elizabeth Rutland was picking at her embroidery and chattering. "Roger says they'll meet no opposition. And there hasn't been any noise of fighting in the streets."

"Nor any sound of jubilation either," said her mother in a low voice.

Penelope suspected that Frank disapproved of the whole undertaking, though if she did, her devotion to Robin would never allow her to say so.

The morning dragged on and it was dinner-time. They could hardly swallow a mouthful from the rich dishes that were served with the usual pomp and tasted of sawdust. Sir John Davies interrupted the meal, concerned about his prisoners.

"Would it please you to come to them, madam? They are getting very restive. I've had meat and wine taken in to them, but they keep demanding to be set free, and the Earl can't mean to detain them there all day. If your ladyship would talk to them . . . "

"How can I talk to them?" asked Frank. "In such a situation what am I to say?"

266

"What does the gracious hostess say when she's got the Lord Keeper — and the Great Seal — locked up in her husband's study? I fear the rules of ceremony won't give us any guidance." Penelope laid down her napkin and stood up. "Come and do your duty, my dear. It's one way we can help his lordship, for these are all honest men, they aren't included among those he means to prosecute, and he won't want an abiding quarrel with any of them."

It was not easy to sail into the study, heads high and lips curved in careful smiles. The prisoners were humped round the chimney-piece in a state of sulky exhaustion which suggested that there had been a good deal of recrimination. Essex had made them look perfect fools — four grown men to fall into such a trap. The servant with the Great Seal was sitting on a stool at the far end of the room, wearing a martyred expression. The fire was smoking.

Egerton levered himself out of his chair. "I'm glad to see you at last, Lady Essex. I trust you can offer us some explanation of your husband's scandalous behaviour."

Frank said, rather faintly, that her husband had thought it wise to take precautions for their lordships' safety. The Lord Chief Justice snorted. Penelope, ignoring the overtones, enquired after her uncle's gout. Was he going to take the waters at Buxton? He was fond of her, he unbent slightly, and Worcester chimed in, asking whether she had ever visited Bath. It was fantastic, this staid exchange of civilities while they all hid the same preoccupation: how many men had Essex mustered in the city? Couldn't he have sent them a reassuring word? And surely he ought to have passed the house again by now, on his march to Whitehall? Penelope talked on, grateful to Worcester for his kindness and good breeding. Though all the unwilling guests seemed more cordial, even the Judge. Penelope was used to the effects of her own beauty, but this was not the ordinary male reaction. They were humouring her with an odd sort of delicacy, almost as though they were sorry for her.

There were movements in the gallery. Penelope caught them before the others; she murmured an excuse and slipped out. At the head of the stairs she saw Meyrick and Davies with a third man, Sir Ferdinando Gorges, who had gone on the expedition to the City. He was breathing hard and mopping the sweat from his beard.

As she walked towards them, her perception slid through all the gradations of hope and doubt to one dreadful certainty. This was disaster.

"Has there been heavy fighting? My brother?"

"Sound enough in health, madam; he'll be here anon. Fighting? One short brush. They wouldn't fight him, but they wouldn't follow him either, curse their craven souls."

"Who wouldn't follow him? The rich merchants? I know the citizens . . . "

"The citizens came out to gape as we went by, but they wouldn't stir. They heard the Earl's appeal like so many logs of wood. All the way down Fleet Street we plodded, by the Poultry to Lombard Street and Fenchurch, and not one solitary prentice took a step to join us. Not one."

The words tumbled out, sense lagging

behind. It was incredible.

"But Sheriff Smythe," said Meyrick. "He was to furnish a thousand halberdiers."

"I'm telling you, we went to Smythe's house, and he crept out and ran squealing to the Lord Mayor. We stayed some time in his house, while the Earl pondered what he should do. Then we got warning that Cecil's brother Burleigh was going round the City with a herald, proclaiming Essex a traitor. We set out again. They were calling up the train-bands; his lordship saw we were lost if we stayed there, and resolved to come home by Ludgate. But we were cut off, they'd got chains across the road. There was an exchange of shot, and young Tracy, his lordship's page, fell dead at his feet."

That was the boy who had gone out so merrily, four hours ago, on his first adventure. His only adventure.

Gorges continued the grim recital. "We tried to charge the barrier, but they were too strong for us. Kit Blount was wounded in the head. We had to leave him behind us when we ran."

Kit — her mother's husband and Charles's cousin. What would they say?

(But what would Charles say to any of this hideous nightmare?)

"So we turned tail and made for Queenhithe," ended Gorges. "The river being still open to us, and our number much depleted. I came ahead in the first boat, to release the Councillors and convey them to the Palace. Those are his lordship's orders, Sir John. There's nothing to gain by holding them now."

Penelope moved away, isolated from what was going on around her; the Councillors leaving with Gorges, the wretched story being repeated to Frank. She was groping through the shock towards a horrifying reality. They thought they had counted all the risks: defeat in a fair fight against superior forces, or treachery from some of the clever time-servers. One factor they had never considered, the citizens' loyalty to their hero. The common people had lapped him in adoration since he was nineteen, gone mad with joy over his victories, wept in the streets when they thought he was dying. Why had they changed? They couldn't all be cowards. And what could Robin have felt? Trudging those weary miles between the indifferent faces, his venture crumbling into the most pitiful failure, abortive and ridiculous. Penelope knew that their cause was ruined, there would be worse ordeals to come, yet she could think only of Robin's anguish when the Londoners rejected him.

She tried to collect her wits. She ought to be comforting Frank instead of mooning here. Outside the study she paused, as the familiar footsteps came up the stairs.

He was haggard, beaten, his mouth drawn taut as a wire in the effort to hide his feelings. But he could not hide the hurt, lost look in his eyes, and his hands were shaking. Penelope did not know how she saw these things, because she was pretending to fumble with the latch. She could not bear to intrude on his privacy in this moment of desolation. He came up behind her, shoved open the study door, and stopped.

"Where are my prisoners?"

"Gorges took them to the Palace, my lord," said John Davies. "He told us — I understood that was your lordship's command."

"Oh God! Then I'm finished indeed. I meant to hold them as hostages."

Poor Davies began to apologise. Robin merely said that Gorges was one more false friend who had found a good method of saving his skin. He did not seem surprised. Taking no notice of his wife and sister, he went to an iron chest and pulled out a bundle of letters.

"What are you doing?" asked Frank.

"Burning my papers."

He threw a sheaf of them on the fire, the embers leapt into a hectic brightness and the smooth white surfaces smudged and darkened, curling over like ferns. Frank and Penelope dragged more bundles from the chest. There were lists here of all his secret well-wishers, and the whole of the Scottish correspondence. Was this Robin's final action before giving himself up? They must find out what he meant to do — if only he didn't look so wretched. Penelope glanced at Frank, who shook her head. They were spared the necessity of asking by the arrival of Southampton.

"Robert, am I to fortify the house?"

"We agreed to it, didn't we? Yes, you are to fortify the house. Do I have to tell you everything three times over?"

Southampton very nearly worshipped Robin; he had seldom received a sharp word from him. He faltered at the savagery behind that retort, but said, "I'll put the work in hand, my lord."

"Better tackle the Strand entrance first." Robin tore through a thick parchment scroll. "Take whatever you need to close up every chink. And Harry . . . "

"My lord?"

"I'm sorry I spoke harshly. I've brought down enough trouble on you without that."

The old magic shone again, in that swift compunction.

"I don't care a fig for my troubles. You know that. You know I'd gladly die for you." Harry had always been theatrical.

"You may have to die with me, if all else fails." But the rigid look on Robin's face had gone, and he was now able to speak candidly to the two women. "You know what I've done, don't you? I've destroyed myself, and my family, and my friends. And you haven't reproached me for it . . . Sweetheart, are you willing to endure the rigours of a siege? I can countermand the order."

"And let them come and take you from me?" There was an inflexible quality about Frank. "This is our home; under God's providence, we'll stay here together as long as we can." She might have added, like Harry, that she would gladly die for Robin, but she had never paraded her feelings, and he did not need to be told.

Penelope knew that the defence of Essex House was a forlorn hope; in spite of that, her spirits had risen. Robin was not beaten yet.

She and Frank finished burning the confidential papers, while Robin went to superintend the men who were turning his house into a citadel. All the solid furniture was piled against the doors and windows of the ground floor. They filled in the gaps with stacks of books, the priceless contents of Robin's library, and wedged the toppling barricades with cushions and curtains and Persian carpets. The denuded rooms, their outer walls deeply reinforced, took on mysterious, unknown shapes in the yellow candlelight. On the upper floors they posted guards with muskets. Men were trampling everywhere, sweating and clumsy in their haste, leaving a trail of torn hangings and broken ornaments. The domestic elegance of years was dissipated in one winter afternoon.

The gentlewomen and maidservants, driven from their vulnerable rooms over the Strand, were herded into the south gallery, providing a discordant note of nervous alarm. Frank set some of them to cutting up sheets for bandages, and chivvied others into the kitchen. They must make gallons of nourishing broth. Ought they to start baking bread? No one knew if they would be there in the morning to eat it.

It was dusk. They would soon know what forces the Council had rounded up to deal with them. (Like Nuts-in-May, thought Penelope, with a defiant flippancy. 'Who shall we send to fetch him away?') Presently the watchers upstairs reported a troop of horsemen in the road. There were creakings and splashings at the landing-stage, and the enemy were in the garden. They were surrounded. Thundering bangs on the door, and a demand that they should open in the Queen's name and yield up the person of Robert, Earl of Essex, on a charge of high treason. No one bothered to reply. A short pause, then much clanking about on the cobbles. Besiegers and defenders called to each other through the darkness, information spread, and they soon knew pretty well who was outside. Lord Cumberland and Tom Howard led the contingent in the Strand. The Lord Admiral, who was in command, had come by water with another party, including his son Effingham, Fulke Greville and Robert Sidney.

"My Uncle Robert," said Elizabeth Rutland.

All their old friends. They had not considered what kind of a siege this would be.

Still no attack. They were wondering at the delay, when a rumour got into the house which explained it. The Lord Admiral was waiting for the cannon to arrive from the Tower.

This started a panic among the women. Hand-to-hand fighting was bad enough, but cannon — they would blow a great, gashing hole in the wall, the ceilings would fall in, or the timbers would catch fire, and they would all perish in the flames. As these horrible ideas burst on them, the sentinels started shooting from the windows; it was too much for the serving-women, who began to wail and lament, some of them praying aloud, others shrieking hysterically. This threatened to demoralise the whole garrison.

"Let me out of here! Let me out!" A fat chambermaid blundered across the gallery, stupid with terror. "Save me, save me, or I'll burn!"

"Hold your tongue, you silly bitch!"

Penelope gave the creature a satisfying slap, which reduced her cries to a whimper. But they were infectious. Penelope had never been so mortified by the feebleness of her sex. Their screams must he audible in the garden.

Apparently they were. Someone came forward with a torch and a white flag. Sir Robert Sidney wished to parley with the Earl or one of his Lieutenants. Southampton went out on the leads to confer with him. When he returned, Robin was in the gallery with his family.

"He had a message from the Lord

Admiral," Harry reported. "If you wish to send the ladies and their attendants out of the house before he attacks, he will grant them a safe passage."

"But every door is barricaded," objected Penelope. "No one can get out, unless we make a breach in the defences. And that's unthinkable."

"So I told him. But he said that if we opened one of the doors, they would give us an hour's grace to close it up again."

Fair chances for all, thought Penelope, as though they were playing tennis. And they'd keep their extraordinary pact. No wonder foreigners laugh at us.

Robin said, "It's a generous offer. You had better take it, Frank."

"My dear lord, don't send me away."

Frank was sitting on a cushion beside her two small daughters — the boy was away at Eton. Frances Devereux could just stagger about, fractious because she was teething. The tiny Dorothy lay in her cradle, placidly awake, her eyes as blue as jewels. She was five weeks old. Frank reached over to tuck in her shawl; her hand trembled. Only now, when there was a chance of escape, did she seem to grasp what was going to happen to her little girls if they stayed. Penelope watched her struggling with the tragic division of love.

"There's a simple solution," she said. "Those who choose shall go, taking the children with them. Lady Essex and I can remain."

"It's not so simple," said Harry. "The Lord Admiral is acting from prudence rather than mercy. He doesn't want to figure as a butcher of the innocent. The safe passage is for all of you or none."

"Well, I won't go," muttered Penelope.

She was conscious that the women had quietened and were directing their combined hopes at her in a wordless entreaty. Some of them were very young; there was a little laundress, so pretty and so frightened — could she condemn that child to the onslaught of the Tower cannon? Or Elizabeth, Philip Sidney's daughter, who was only sixteen? Or the two babies? Frank would give in and go, because she was their mother. And I'm a mother too, thought Penelope, though she had refused all day to think of her darlings in the safe world outside.

Little Frances had been sucking her coral; she dropped it and began to cry. She probably had toothache, but the pathetic sound unnerved her father.

"Lord Southampton, you may tell Sir Robert that I am thankful to accept the Lord Admiral's gesture of compassion." And then, very softly, to Penelope, "You must do as I tell you, and go. Otherwise I shall surrender."

There was no more to be said.

Southampton went out on the roof again; a posse of men started to dismantle the barrier at one of the garden doors. The women servants scurried about collecting a few possessions to take with them. Elizabeth and Roger Rutland sat in a corner, holding hands.

And Robin paced up and down, saying in a tired, husky voice that they would give a good account of themselves; the citizens would come to their senses when they saw how he was beleaguered by his enemies. They would rescue him. Or if not, he and his companions would fight their way out, get down to Greenwich and commandeer a ship. When he reached France or Scotland he would send for

Frank and they would be reunited and happy. They none of them believed these fairy-tales. Robin was quite aware that they were getting out so that he could make the only free decision left to him: he could die like a Devereux and not like a criminal.

The men had got through to the door. It was time to go. Penelope was so overwhelmed that she could not yet experience the full impact of pain. There were no tears, they were petrified to a dull ache inside her. She embraced her brother, and heard his broken whisper, "May God be with you always — my dearest Penelope." She hardly knew what she answered, too poignantly aware of the warmth and substance of his actual presence, the physical splendour, and the charm that survived even in defeat. Everything essential to Robin was still there — for how much longer? A matter of hours or days, it made no difference.

She knew that she would never see him again.

But she pressed his fingers, and walked away without turning, while he said good-bye to Frank.

The women were congregated at the buttery door. The three peeresses went out ahead of their attendants. Frank insisted on carrying the baby, Elizabeth was clasping her other little half-sister. Penelope, choking in the night air, braced herself to meet the stern condemnation of the loyal subjects who had come to put down a rebellion. The severity probably tinged with contempt, because this rebellion had been such a poor futile thing, not much more than a riot.

But it was not like that. There was no hostility and certainly no triumph. Fulke Greville and Robert Sidney came forward bareheaded to escort them to the boats. They looked so sad, everyone looked sad. They might have been on the losing side. In spite of themselves, they had to win. Incorruptible, they were doing their duty and hating it.

In the end there was no fighting. A blind instinct of the outcast and the hunted had made the rebels bar themselves into their only haven. But when the first impetus had gone, their ardour chilled. Officers and men alike had been too disheartened by that terrible march through the City; they had lost faith in their leader, and they wanted to throw themselves on the Queen's mercy. Nothing Essex could do would persuade them to stand firm.

So at ten o'clock that night he came out into the garden, knelt in submission to the Lord Admiral, and gave up his sword.

Next morning he was taken down the Thames and into the Tower of London by the Traitors' Gate.

3

PENELOPE was in the Fleet Prison. They were all in prison, the ringleaders: Harry and Roger in the Tower, like Robin, as well as five other lords, Henry Cuffe, and Kit, who had been wounded and captured in the City. Frank and Elizabeth were free; even the Queen saw them as devoted wives rather than conspirators. Penelope did not envy them. Any place would be a prison now, and if anything she was consoled by her uncomfortable distinction.

She wondered if they would send her to the block. Being a woman was no safeguard; there was Mary Stuart, Jane Grey, Anne Boleyn ... She hoped she could die as well as they had — if only she could control a fastidious horror as she imagined her head rolling away like a football soaked in blood, and all the people staring. That picture made her throat contract so that she could not swallow.

She tried not to think of her family, the little ones needing her so badly — St. John was not quite two. They would be the worst sufferers, Charles's children; what would become of them if she died? As for Charles, it was unbearable to think of him, and the agonies of suspense he must be going through, over in Ireland. Confused with all the love and longing and regret was the knowledge that Charles had been right about Cecil. The Secretary of State was quite innocent of any treason or plotting with Spain.

This came out at Robin's trial. He and Harry were tried together, in St. Stephen's Hall at Westminster, before a Commission of their peers. Penelope got a full account of the trial from her gaolers, who were filled with pity for their beautiful prisoner.

Robin put up a most gallant fight. Not for his life. It was obvious that he expected to die and did not much care. But he did care passionately that his honour should be cleared. He had not acted from a greedy, selfish ambition; he had not intended to depose the Queen and seize the Crown for himself. No need to say that he had meant to use her as a puppet and to rule in her name, that would be misinterpreted; the point was that he had acted entirely for her good, and for the good of her subjects. He resented the cheap attacks on his patriotism, and he resented still more being called a papist and an atheist. (How he could be both at the same time, no one bothered to explain.) It was Cecil who conspired with papists, Ralegh who was the atheist; they were the villains who should stand in his place. Robin was determined that everyone should recognise him as a man who had been driven to break the law from the highest motives. He was also determined, if it was humanly possible, to save Southampton.

So, with these two aims, he fought back, quick-witted, fluent, and sometimes decidedly aggressive, against the insults of the Attorney-General, and the deadly, insinuating logic of his old friend Francis Bacon. It warmed Penelope to know that Robin had risen above his despair to display the full force of his vivid personality.

Everyone was disgusted, her informants

told her, by Mr. Bacon's callous prosecution of his benefactor, but he had done less harm than his cousin, Sir Robert Cecil. When the Spanish plot was mentioned, little Cecil popped out from behind a curtain, where he had been hiding all the time, shrill with indignation. It was more like a play than a court of law, they said. Cecil wanted a public vindication, and the form of the trial took a strange turn, for it was now Cecil's words and conduct that came under scrutiny, witnesses were called, and a sobering fact emerged: the stories that Robin had believed about Cecil were nothing but the wildest fabrication.

This was a shock. (Just how much of a shock to the rebels' consciences, it would take some time to realise.) Robin had rallied from it, strong in his own innocence, and convinced that Cecil had deliberately set out to ruin him, from sheer malice. He held his head as high as ever.

The trial ended. The peers retired, and when they filed in again, The Lord High Steward had required each of them to stand up separately and say " . . . Whether is Robert, Earl of Essex, guilty of this treason whereupon he has been indicted, or no?" The answer was never in doubt, yet it must have been like the repeated lashing of a whip for a sensitive man to have the verdict proclaimed twenty-five times over: "Guilty, my lord, of high treason, upon mine honour."

Southampton was also found guilty. There was only one sentence for high treason, though the prisoners were then asked if they would petition the Queen for mercy.

Robin refused. "I owe God a death," he said simply. He was anxious that the lords should not mistake this for pride. "I do crave Her Majesty's mercy, with all humility, yet I would rather die than live in misery."

He saved his pleading for Southampton, and Southampton was extremely ready to plead for himself. Not so keen now to share Robin's fate. Well, he was young and gay, pining for his pretty wife and the carefree pleasures they had enjoyed together, "Rough winds do shake the darling buds of May, and summer's lease hath all too short a date." How well Shakespeare had observed the texture of his patron's disposition. Penelope, mulling it all over in her prison, could not blame Harry for being what he was. But she knew a better kind of man. The valiant Icarus, the winged hero, having soared and fallen, would not make terms with failure and disgrace, because he wanted only perfection.

His gift for friendship, at least, was indestructible. After the sentence, she was told, as he and Southampton were taken away, with the sharp edge of the axe towards them, Robin had stopped beside Lord De La Warr and Lord Morley, to say how sorry he was for having led their sons into trouble. The selfless care for others, at such a moment, was the very quality which had drawn those two boys, and so many more, like a lodestar.

Now it was the 25th February, Ash Wednesday. Penelope sat in her cell, gazing up at the segment of sky outside the high, barred window, and trying to project her mind that short distance to the Tower so that she could know the exact minute when the thread of Robin's life snapped, as his neck snapped under the axe. How iniquitous it seemed, the abolition of a breathing, healthy, active man. He was only thirty-three. She could visualise the setting: that horrible bare patch on Tower Green where the grass wouldn't grow. And the sombre ravens, haunting the place like the reproaches of the dead. Yet it was a concession of the Queen's to let him die there in comparative privacy; normally traitors were beheaded outside the walls, on Tower Hill. Robin was the first person to die on Tower Green who was not of royal blood ... Surely it must be over by now? My sweet Robin, if only you are safe and free.

There were footsteps nearing her door, a portentous rattle of bolts and chains. The Chief Warder had promised to bring her the news.

But it was a visitor from outside; Tom Howard, the Constable of the Tower.

She looked at him. It was difficult to move her lips.

"Is he — is it all done?"

"An hour ago. I came as soon as I could, didn't want you to hear it from strangers." Howard was also finding it hard to speak. "He died very bravely, as we all knew he would."

Penelope felt a spasm of actual pain which made her giddy. Howard fetched her a cup of water from the small table. After a few sips, she murmured that it was kind of him to come. It was kind, from a high Officer of State to a rebel awaiting judgment. But his own father, the Duke of Norfolk, had been executed when Tom was a boy of eleven. He sat on the bed — she had the only chair — and began a leisurely account of Robin's last hour, understanding that it was better to know the worst than guess about it.

"There were about a hundred persons assembled; all reluctantly, I may say, but brought by their formal duties. The general sorrow was very heavy; most of us had hoped — that is, many people believed that Her Majesty would never bring herself to sign the warrant."

"I had no doubt of it," said Penelope flatly. What a lot of fools there were who still thought the Queen was capable of genuine love. At least her victim's sister had been spared any false hopes. "You say the sorrow was general, my lord. Where was Cecil, then? And Ralegh?"

"Cecil remained at Court. Ralegh was there, but this affronted some of the gentlemen, who suggested he had come to gloat. In which I think they were unjust. However, Ralegh took himself into the armoury, out of sight.

"Essex was brought out, accompanied by that little chaplain of his, Ashton, who's been with him all along, and two other divines. Dressed entirely in black, among the Guard in their martial array, he still looked more soldierly than any of them. And there was something more: a most wonderful dignity and calm. We could see that he was praying. He mounted the scaffold, and began his speech — his confession." Howard hesitated, running his thumb along the pattern of the quilt.

"I don't think I wish to hear of my brother's confession."

Penelope detested this baring of the soul that was considered an essential part of every execution. She thought it unseemly and often downright unctuous. Not that Robin had anything startling to confess, except, she supposed, a certain contrition because he was technically guilty of treason. And of course his private sins: those endless adventures with women. Old history now, but a dying man must acknowledge the whole of his past. She certainly did not want to hear about it.

Howard seemed thankful to skip the confession. "He was quite brief; none of the flourishes we sometimes hear. Then he spoke to the executioner, and forgave him — you know the ritual. One of the clergy counselled him not to be afraid, and he said he had been so often in danger, and knew only too well how fear could work on him, but he hoped God would strengthen him now. And that's a strange thing," said Howard, digressing, "I never saw him show the slightest flicker of weakness, not in the cold, grim lull before an attack, nor yet in the most desperate carnage. And neither did anyone else. It was always the same; when you served with Essex, you had to push yourself beyond your limit, even to follow where his courage led. We thought him fearless; if he was as frightened as the rest of us — well, it makes me esteem his valour more than ever."

Penelope felt the hot tears under her eyelids.

Howard sighed. "Where was I? Yes. He took off his wrought velvet gown and his ruff, and knelt down, asking us to pray with him. He implored God 'to assist me in this my last combat', recited the Creed, and prayed for his enemies with infinite charity. And when we joined in the Lord's Prayer, Essex broke off in the middle and said a second time, slowly, 'As we forgive them that trespass against us'."

It could not have been easy for Robin to forgive his enemies. Remembering his black storms of hatred in the last few months, she was relieved that he had managed it. Which of them, she wondered, had caused the last struggle implicit in that repeated phrase.

"And then," said Howard, "he took off his doublet and stood before us in his scarlet waistcoat. He bowed to the block, and said, 'O God, I prostrate myself to my deserved punishment'."

Deserved punishment? Well, there was Christian humility for you.

"He lay down in the straw, and put his

head — do you wish me to go on?"

"Yes."

"He made himself ready and prayed a little longer, very softly. The first few verses of the Miserere. Then he stretched his arms in the agreed signal, and called out, 'Executioner, strike home!' And still we heard his voice, firm and true: 'Come, Lord Jesus. Come, Lord Jesus. O Lord, into Thy hands I commend my spirit'."

Howard stopped speaking. The change from sound to silence in that little room seemed as definite as the change from flesh and blood to that other element which had received Robin in a flash, in the twinkling of an eye, and where he was now, surely, with God. In that more glorious world he would live for ever. There was nothing left of him on this earth; only a gaping emptiness that no one could fill.

Penelope forced herself to ask for one ugly detail.

"How many times did the headsman . . . "

"Three times. But he never stirred, even at the first blow. I assure you, he did not suffer."

"How can you say that?" She shivered.

"He admitted that he was afraid, he had to lie down in the straw, like an animal, and tell that man to kill him . . . "

"The word was ill-chosen; I was thinking of bodily pain. I can't deny that he has suffered greatly, one way and another, in the last few days, yet he found peace at last — or the certainty of peace ahead. Did I tell you that we received the Sacrament together? I was very touched that he should want me with him. And I never knew a man with a more complete and loving faith in God."

"He had that from a child."

"It carried him through triumphantly at the end. I believe he was the only man on Tower Green who did not shed a tear. The rest of us, his lifelong friends, his brothers-in-arms, we could hardly stand by and watch that hideous tragedy. That it should be Essex of all men — I'm sorry. What a selfish dolt I am, playing on your grief. But it's the same everywhere; not a smile or a greeting in the streets this morning. London's like a graveyard. Except," amended Howard, "just round the Tower. When the executioner left, the Sheriffs were obliged to rescue him from the fury of the crowd. They tried to tear him in pieces."

The crowd, thought Penelope, would have done better to fight for their beloved Earl when he needed them, instead of storing up their violence for his executioner. It would be wrong to say so to the Constable of the Tower, who had already expressed some remarkable views on the death of a convicted traitor. So the people were mourning? And what were they doing at Court — dancing? Not that it mattered what outsiders felt or did. This was her sorrow.

"Did Robin leave a letter for me?" she asked, firmly confident that he would have written.

"No, there was no letter. None for Lady Essex either, or your mother."

Poor Robin, too wretched even to say goodbye. The thought tore at her heart. She did not think she could ever be more unhappy.

A few hours later she found that she was wrong.

4

THAT evening Penelope received two other visitors: the Lord Admiral and Sir Robert Cecil. Having cried too much, and eaten too little, she now had the feverish sensation that there were layers of wool separating her mind from her body, and her body from the ground. She stood up, resentful that they could not leave her alone for even one day — but perhaps she had no claim to the ordinary observances of mourning. So she curtsied to the Lord Admiral, and waited.

Both men had the grace to apologise for coming.

"We were very loth to break in on you tonight, madam," said Lord Nottingham. "However, we are here on the Queen's business, which cannot be delayed. It is necessary that Mr. Secretary and I should ask you certain questions. But you may be seated."

Penelope sat on the bed this time,

leaving the chair for the Lord Admiral. Cecil leant his hunched frame lightly against the table. She noticed that he was holding some papers.

"This examination," began Nottingham, "concerns some new evidence we have received since your brother's trial. While he was in the Tower, awaiting execution, Lord Essex wrote and signed a confession . . . "

"Signed a confession!" repeated Penelope, forgetting to be submissive. "I don't believe it!"

For it must be nonsense. A confession to God on the scaffold, yes. All men are sinners. But a political document, such as Nottingham implied — that was quite impossible.

"Nevertheless, it is true," said Cecil. "I have it here, written in his own hand."

"Let me see it," she demanded. "What does it say? What is he supposed to have confessed?"

"Chiefly his wickedness in stirring up a rebellion against the Crown, and in planning to seize and intimidate Her Majesty while he usurped her sacred power." Cecil began to read, precisely and without any emphasis. "*I must confess that I am the greatest, the most vile, and most unthankful traitor that was ever born . . .* " The admissions poured out: he had lied at his trial, he had intended all along to depose the Queen in fact, though not in law, and to become the real master of her kingdom. He had made false accusations against Cecil and Ralegh. He had been willing to plunge his country into civil war; he was thankful that God had thwarted his sinful purpose, and made him an example. Penelope was so stunned by this avalanche of self-abasement that she had heard a page of it before she managed to interrupt.

"It's a forgery. Essex never wrote that craven stuff. Here, let me see."

She jumped up, grabbing the papers out of Cecil's hand. He let them go, but hovered very close in case she tried to destroy them.

She skimmed the lines, frantically. It was not a forgery. This was Robin's writing, it was unmistakable. And the style was authentic even though it was perverted into this abject, guilty grovelling. How had they made him do

301

it? Surely they would not have dared to torture a nobleman, the Queen's cousin? Or had his ordeal driven him mad? He had walked on to Tower Green, in front of a hundred witnesses, sane and straight. Things that Tom Howard had said, or left unsaid, struck her now. The surprise that Robin had left no farewell letters, the meek acceptance of a 'deserved punishment', and his last prayer, the agonising fifty-first psalm. Bewildered, she went on searching through his statement.

A sentence leapt out of the text and hit her. She gasped, and knew that the two men had stiffened in expectation. This was the crux of it, the reason they had come.

And now I must accuse one who is most nearest to me, my sister, who did continually urge me on with telling me how all my friends and followers thought me a coward, and that I had lost my valour. She must be looked to, for she has a proud spirit.

It was unbelievable. Yet there were the words: cold, heartless and condemning. And even then the load of blame, which might very well cost her life, was not enough, apparently. In this catalogue of crimes against the State he had seen fit to include the scandal which had hung over her for nine years. This had nothing remotely to do with treason, and everyone knew about it anyway, which somehow made the allusion still more horrible. As though she was so sunk in vice that her own brother could not mention her without dragging in her notorious and persistent adultery with Lord Mountjoy.

All her defences broke in that moment of grief and degradation.

"Robin, how could you?" she sobbed. "Oh, Robin, how could you be so cruel?"

Her inquisitors shifted uneasily. The Lord Admiral was muttering in his beard. "For a gentleman to denounce his sister in such a manner! Don't wish to malign the dead — and he made a brave end. But this sticks in my gullet as much as his treason."

Penelope was not listening. Hiding herself as well as she could in the shadow of the bed-curtain, she was too much ashamed to face the men who had seen those humiliating phrases. To gain time and composure, she pretended to go on reading, picking up an impression here and there. He had attacked Henry Cuffe too. And Kit, their stepfather. Then Mountjoy's name again, and her heart froze, for this was the worst betrayal of all. The rest of his friends had been implicated in the rising, and the Council knew it. But here Robin had dredged up a secret which need never have come to light: Charles's proposal, a year ago, that he should get rid of Cecil and force the Queen to appoint her successor, by coming back from Ireland with the army at his heels.

Everything else was swallowed up in terror.

"What will they do to Mountjoy?" she asked, piteous and trembling.

"Nothing," said the Lord Admiral.

Cecil coughed.

"It's no good your coughing at me, Sir Robert," said the old man. "What passes here is between these four walls, but I will not have Lady Rich subjected to groundless torments. She is already being sufficiently punished for any wrong she may have done. Take courage, child." He spoke as he might have spoken, years ago, to the pretty little cousin who came to play with his daughter. "When you can reflect more calmly, you will see that the very last thing we want is to find fault with Mountjoy, or to remove him from his present command. If he made any wild plans, they perished in his brain, and he certainly played no part in the rebellion. Do you think Her Majesty is going to proceed against the best general she ever had? The only man in forty years who's proved himself a match for the Irish?"

Penelope was still too frightened to be logical. She shot a glance at the little hunchback whom she feared most as an enemy.

He responded with a diffident kindness, the Secretary of State allowing himself a mild indiscretion. "I think it can do no harm to tell your ladyship this: we sent a despatch to Ireland on Monday; that was after Her Majesty had read Lord Essex's confession. I asked her, in the customary way, if she had any particular matter to raise with the Lord Deputy. She dictated a trifling message, using terms of the warmest affection. That was all."

So Charles was safe.

"I thank you, Sir Robert," she said. "It is generous of you to give me that comfort, after the treatment you have received from — some of my family." Her political acumen was reviving. "You must know that all these stories are pure fancy. I can only think my poor brother was moved by envy of Lord Mountjoy's victories." It seemed the one explanation of Robin's monstrous treachery towards them both. Crushed by the pain of it, she still retained an instinct to defend herself for Charles's sake, because she was the real link between him and the rebels. The more guilt they piled on her, the more people would suspect him of being an accessary. "I never had any influence over Essex in his decisions. Everyone knows I was more like a slave than a sister. I worked and toiled for him, and did what I was told. And that was not by reason of his authority," she ended sadly, "but simply out of love."

An honest, generous trusting love that death had not quenched. Was it only this morning she had wept, because he

306

had gone out of her reach? She had not valued what still belonged to her then: the proud and happy memories. Now he had poisoned the past. Everything was twisted out of shape in the distorting-glass of his final judgment. She would never dare to look back. She had lost Robin as though he had never existed.

Nottingham and Cecil still had to question her, but they were very gentle. By a paradox, Robin's confession had helped; they wanted to be lenient. Everyone was lenient, even the Queen, for a few days later Penelope was set free. The Queen, having overlooked her Lord Deputy's misdemeanours, was not going to distract his attention from the war by prosecuting his mistress. This did not occur to Penelope, she was not interested in her release. She would rather have died.

She went to Stratford-le-Bow; Rich and the children were there. Rich had served on the Commission at Robin's trial, and she had felt then that she could never speak to him again — a man who would condemn his brother-in-law. Now she had discovered there were darker shades of infamy; it was hardly worth despising Rich.

Stratford looked familiar yet foreign, seen through tear-stretched eyes and the blur of a perpetual headache. It was she who was foreign, an entirely different person from the petted and triumphant favourite sister of the greatest man in England. I will not think of him, she told herself for the hundredth time, as she got wearily out of the coach.

Her children had assembled to meet her; she had forgotten they would all be dressed in black. The four youngest rushed forward, hugging her with delight. Harry and Charles, the middle ones, bowed ceremoniously and tried to look nonchalant, but they couldn't keep it up. They had been so frightened while she was in prison. They hugged her too. Above the tumbling babies and the excited clamour, Penelope saw her three eldest: Lettice, Essex and Robert. She kissed their smooth young cheeks, and heard their murmured greetings, a cross between condolence and congratulation. Having hoped the girls would not break down, it was a little blighting to find them so self-possessed. To find they were shutting her out with a wall of reserve that had never been there before.

Had they turned against her too? Siding with their father, who presumably thought she was a traitor? (They could not know about the confession; the Council were sitting on that, embarrassed by the reference to Mountjoy.)

"You must be tired, madam," said Lettice, as though speaking to an elderly invalid, and shepherding her upstairs to the great chamber. Essex sent the younger children away, which was a pity, because Penelope could be at ease with them. She was not used to being managed by her daughters, but was too apathetic to protest.

Robert began to talk, stiffly at first, until his tongue ran away with him. "There's a rumour Lord Southampton will be reprieved." He flushed, afraid he had been tactless.

"I hope it may be true," said Penelope steadily. "Your uncle fought so hard to save him."

(He didn't slander Harry, or say he had a proud spirit . . . I won't think of him.) The children were nervous and awkward. Perhaps they were not hostile, simply overwhelmed by the tragedy. They had no experience of bereavement and did not know how to treat her.

Lettice drew a long breath. "Madam, there's something we think — Essex and Rob and I — something we should tell you." She broke off as the door opened.

"So you've come," said Rich.

"Yes, I've come."

Rich did not change, she thought, except to grow redder and thicker — and richer. She could not deal with him now.

"I think I'll go to bed," she said. "Or perhaps I'll have a bath." That was a good idea. For the first time since the rising she had thought of something she would like to do, a fragmentary relief. "I'll have a bath, and then I'll get into my own bed and sleep for a week."

"Not in this house," said Rich.

"Why not? It's my home, isn't it? Or would your lordship prefer me to go and hide my head at Leez? It might be more prudent."

"Neither here not at Leez, madam.

310

They are not your houses, they are mine, and you forfeited your right to live in them long ago. Since then you have stayed on sufferance; well, that concession is over. You can lie here tonight, I suppose, and then you can take yourself off, and your tribe of bastards with you. See if you can make Mountjoy feed his brats; likely he'll desert you as he deserted your precious brother. But don't come whining back to me. I've finished with you for good, and I'll not have you corrupting my sons and daughters, inciting them to a life of lust and treason."

He went out, slamming the door.

Penelope had remained perfectly still. She was not capable of any further emotion, only a dull astonishment. And an uncomfortable pounding of her heart. After twenty years, to cast her off in such a way, at such a time — but how exactly like Rich.

The children were very quiet, though they had all moved closer to her chair.

"Did you know he was going to turn me out?"

"Yes, we wanted to warn you." Lettice's voice was choked with distress. "We

311

didn't know how to begin."

So that was the reason for their dreadful constraint, poor lambs. It vanished now, and they clung round her, all talking at once.

"We've pleaded and begged him not to, but he won't listen. He would have done it years ago, only he was afraid of my uncle. Darling, sweet mother, what shall we do without you? . . . He says we may not see you, but if Lettice marries Sir George Carey, we'll go and live with her, and you can come too. He's so much in love, he won't mind."

Poor George Carey.

"If only I was older, I could protect you." With a responsible, man-of-the-family air, Robert added, "I think it would be fitting if I wrote to Lord Mountjoy. But I wish I could take care of you myself."

"Robert did stand up for you most gallantly," put in Essex. "And my father said he was insolent, and beat him for it."

"Poor Robert, I'm sorry." Penelope pressed the martyr's hand.

Watching their loving, loyal faces, she

was stricken to think she had doubted them. She wouldn't have lost faith so easily a week ago.

"Will you go to Wanstead?" Lettice asked her. "I know that's what Lord Mountjoy would wish."

Would he? Her world had been so completely shattered, that Penelope no longer knew what any man would wish. Charles had told her to keep out of the rising, she had ignored his advice, and in the squalid sequel her brother had betrayed his secrets and accused him of treason. Would any man, after that, be willing to have her dumping herself in his house with four children? Well, her dear Charles might; she really did not believe he would fail her. And where else could she go? Not to her mother or Frank, who would want to talk interminably about their dead hero. If only Wanstead was not saturated with Robin's presence too. It was like being in a cage, barred in, whichever way she turned, by bitter memories.

"It will have to be Wanstead," she said slowly. "For a start. And the little ones are always happy there."

"I wish we could come with you," said Essex dolefully. "I wish I was one of your Blounts. I shouldn't mind being a bastard if I had Lord Mountjoy for a father."

"I'm sure you should not say so," cautioned the more mature Lettice.

"Why not? It's true. He's kind and brave and handsome, and I admire him more than anyone except — more than any man living. And who used to boast that she was Philip Sidney's daughter? Yes, you did, Letty — until you read *Astrophel* and found out you couldn't be."

Penelope heard them with an unpleasant pricking of her conscience. Had she really corrupted her children? Through being the kind of woman whose brother described her as a wanton to the Privy Council?

"No more of that," she said sharply. "You are both Lord Rich's daughters, and you'll be wise to remember it, unless you want to starve."

"But we all look thorough Devereux," remarked Robert. "Everyone says so."

They all looked thorough Devereux, especially Robert, whose enchanting smile had belonged to that other sweet-tempered boy so long ago. Suddenly Penelope began to cry. The children tried hard to console her, saying all the wrong things because, of course, they did not understand what she was really crying about.

Part Five

The Lord Deputy

March 1602

1

HER MAJESTY's Viceroy of
Ireland, called home for discussions with the Council, walked
through the Privy Gallery with the
Secretary of State. It was two years since
he had been at Court, and there were
many changes. The most obvious — he
could hardly get away from it — was
the changed attitude towards himself.
Charles Mountjoy knew that he had
been well liked, but he had not aspired
for anything more, living close to those
greater and more dazzling than himself,
a well-mannered and moderate frog in
a big puddle. He had never expected
to find himself the largest frog in the
pond. Surrounded by enthusiastic friends
who wanted to wring his hand, wide-
eyed beauties who wanted a conqueror
to worship, politicians who wanted his
opinion as they never had before,
sycophants who wanted to lick his
boots — that was nauseating, but it

was the surest sign of success. The sign of genuine achievement was the respect of men whom he respected, and who recognised him at this precise juncture as the most outstanding man in the State. The victor of Kinsale.

The Spaniards, encouraged by Tyrone, had landed seven thousand men on the coast of Ireland. Mountjoy, making a tremendous effort, had swept across the country to meet them, mewed them up and besieged them in Kinsale Castle. Then he, in his turn, had been encircled by Tyrone. The allied forces, Spanish and Irish, were far stronger than his; they thought they could finish him between them, in a joint attack from each side. That was last Christmas Eve. He had moved too quickly for them, out-manœuvred Tyrone, stolen the best position, and charged with his cavalry to smash the rebel supremacy for good and all. It was a bloody fray. After which the Spaniards had been glad to creep off home. If they ever tried to invade England again, it would not be through the Irish back-door. And Tyrone was no longer a serious menace; he was skulking in the north like an outlaw, poor devil. A few more months of skirmishing would bring him to surrender. The Battle of Kinsale had effectively killed two birds with one stone.

The reserved and unassuming man who had won that battle was not too much puffed up by the courtiers' acclamation. The two whose voices he would have liked to hear were missing; the brother and sister he had secretly longed to impress. One was dead, and the other could never come back to Court while the Queen reigned. And without them, the Palace was a sepulchre.

"Yes, there have been great changes," remarked Cecil, with his uncomfortable flair for mind-reading. "We are very gay — masques and plays every night — but it's not the same. We still miss him. I wouldn't admit as much to anyone save your lordship, but my happiest times were spent in his company, when we were good friends . . . You know we were reconciled before he died? I saw him in the Tower; I shall always be glad of that."

"I am sure it must have lightened his

burden, Sir Robert."

Charles looked down at the little man with the guarded, rather mournful face. At one time he and Cecil would each have been prepared to destroy the other if necessary, but they did not let this interfere with their present alliance, they were both political realists. It was Cecil who had most right to feel resentful, for he had certainly been wronged and slandered by all the Essex faction. He might be ambitious and self-seeking, he had probably rejoiced at his enemy's final overthrow, but he was not a traitor. And neither he nor the Queen had been vindictive.

There had been very little blood spilt after the rising. Charles's cousin Kit had followed his stepson to the block, and there had been three other executions: Cuffe, Danvers and Gelly Meyrick. Southampton was still in prison. Rutland and the other lords had been heavily fined and set free. It had been a merciful end to an episode of tragic futility, yet they were all still suffering from it, and here, as the culminating irony, was Cecil lamenting Essex because he found the world a duller place without him.

They waited at the door of the Privy Chamber until Anthony Killigrew appeared.

"Her Majesty will receive the Lord Deputy alone."

Charles was ushered in to kneel before his Prince.

She's a thousand years old, he thought, shocked by his first sight of her. Absence might have dimmed his memory, but surely she had not been like this when he went away? All the stage-trappings — the wig, the fantastic ruff, the load of jewels — had been there before; now they seemed grotesquely to encase a skeleton. Her flesh had wasted, the bones were dreadfully visible through the paint. Only the eyes were alive and they were the hardest thing about her. She was more like the goddess of a savage tribe than the greatest lady in Europe.

"Mountjoy."

One spoken word, and the image flowered into warmth and animation, even the eyes. With her voice she was still an enchantress. That, and the quality of her mind, triumphed over all the rest. She gave Charles her hand to kiss.

"Mountjoy, you are most welcome. Both for your own sake — and you should know by now how dear you are to us — and for your patient, valiant service to our Realm. There is a true delight in thanking you, for we never had a subject more deserving of thanks and praise."

Charles knew that the royal pronoun signified a very special degree of approval.

"Your Majesty does me too much honour. I can only say that Your Majesty never had a subject who loved you with a more faithful devotion."

This was the correct answer, like following suit at cards. In fact he meant it. And then a disturbing thought pierced him. She had read Robert's confession. She knew that he, like Robert, had played with sedition, ready to come armed into her Palace and compel her to dismiss her Ministers against her will. What exactly could his protests of faithful devotion sound like to her?

He coloured, biting his lip. The Queen smiled, a little ironically. Then he felt the light pressure of her fingers on his shoulder.

"Your loyalty is taken for granted. It is a matter that requires no discussion."

He bowed his head. He knew what she was telling him. The Queen could not entrust an army to a man who had once planned to use it as a threat against herself; she had chosen to treat Robert's accusation as a piece of jealous spite, and she would not hear a definite admission. Charles would have given a great deal, at that moment, to be free to blurt out the whole story, tell her he was sorry, and beg her to forgive him. But he must observe her rule of bland diplomacy. He knew that she had forgiven him, unasked; he had never felt so conscious of real humility in his relations with his Sovereign.

"Tell me how you scoured the pots," she said, in a rallying tone.

He laughed, recovering his poise. He wouldn't be allowed to escape from that. A few months ago, in an unusual fit of self-pity, he had sent a long list of grumbles to Cecil, saying that no one in England took any notice of his despatches or cared what happened to him, he was sick of being treated like a scullion. He was very much disconcerted, when the next post arrived, to get a letter in the Queen's own hand beginning 'Mistress Kitchen-maid', and teasing him for being so cross. She had gone on to praise him in the kind of language she had used this morning. And such a reward, from this marvellous and extraordinary woman, made you want to go out and die for her, or slave yourself to a shadow. (That was something he could never explain to Penelope.) The Queen wanted to hear about Kinsale, and about the long months of preparation and training which had made Kinsale possible. Presently he was in difficulties; it was necessary to mention Robert. He had meant to ask Cecil if this would provoke an outburst. He felt his way by speaking of 'my predecessor'.

"Which of your predecessors?"

"The Earl of Essex, madam."

"The late Earl of Essex," corrected the Queen with a devastating calm. "Continue, my lord."

Charles blinked, and continued. When

he had finished, she asked if there was any request he wished to make, any favour she could show him. Charles wanted the same favour that any soldier wanted after two years in the field: permission to go home to the woman he loved. He did not think the Queen would appreciate this. Cautiously, he hoped he might be allowed a few days' leave, between the Council's deliberations. There were matters needing attention on his estate at Wanstead.

"So you wish to run off and consort with a rebel?"

"Your Majesty has graciously pardoned her. And — I am anxious to see my children."

"You are a bachelor, Mountjoy. You should not have any children, let alone speak of them in my presence."

The Queen had an irritating habit of producing this quite unconvincing note of virginal propriety when it suited her convenience.

"I think Your Majesty knows the circumstances," said Charles. "And that I have four children to whom I owe a special care, because I can give them no legal protection." He thought he saw a way

327

of appeal, through the qualities she valued most. "When my elder daughter was born, madam, the scandal was overlooked for her mother's sake; she was in high esteem then, and had powerful friends. I was of little account in those days; I was poor, and a commoner, with no particular merit or reputation — I could not shield her, it was she who shielded me. Now the case is altered. Your Majesty's gracious confidence has raised me to a high office, and enabled me to do you some service. I have been fortunate. While Lady Rich is alone, disgraced and unhappy. I know how gravely she has sinned against Your Majesty; others may well condemn her, but surely I am the one person who ought not to desert her now? Your Majesty would not think better of a public servant who proved himself so ungrateful in his private dealings."

He saw the painted mouth twist, and stopped, horrified. So pleased with his argument, he had not worked out where it was leading. To a comparison with that other servant whose ingratitude, both public and private, had hurt her so desperately. The man who had called himself the most unthankful traitor that was ever born.

The Queen plucked at the feathers of her fan, frowning, while his chance of seeing Penelope hung in the balance. Then she turned to him, brusquely.

"Very well, you may go to Wanstead. And if you must charge yourself with that wanton and her brats, I'll give you a word of counsel. Be sure that you are a strict father to your sons. We need no more spoilt children from that family."

Again she gave him her hand to kiss. As he took it, her grip tightened, and she drew him closer, and whispered, with a sudden anguish: "Charles, you loved him too, but you understand. I had to do it. He left me no choice." The tears were brimming in the tragic eyes. "I warned him that he must not touch my sceptre. He was so headstrong, he would not learn — Charles I had to do it."

"I know, madam. There was no other way." He spoke very gently, possessed with pity for this old and lonely woman, who had destroyed the man she loved most in the world, because the inviolate supremacy of the Sovereign must always come before human affection. "May I presume to remind Your Majesty that he also understood? He said that you were right. He did learn his lesson, in the end."

At what a terrible cost to them both.

2

"YOU are the same as ever," said Penelope. "Just as I've conjured you up so many times in my imagination; I almost fear you may vanish through the arras. Your lordship never found that doublet in a bog."

She smiled at him across the table. He had arrived at noon, on four days' leave, and they had come straight in to dinner, so she was still getting used to the reality of Charles, with his air of sober magnificence and groomed to a sheen, looking as though he had never been further than five miles from the Court. He said that his Italian tailor had quickly contrived him something fit to wear.

"Military dress is well enough in its place; I am glad to be out of it."

Certainly Charles did not carry the imprint of the camp around with him. You wouldn't expect him to stride through the Palace, his boots caked in mud — automatically, a shutter slammed in Penelope's mind. She went on smiling at Charles, and talking trivialities, because their two elder children, Penny and Isabel, were dining with them. When they were alone it would be different; at present there was a curious constraint. Two years was a long time, and so much had happened. It was thirteen months since the rising, but the violent, unnatural horror of that February haunted her still. She had come to Wanstead when Rich turned her out. Charles's letters had made it plain that he considered himself responsible for her and for their children, so she had stayed, isolated in the Forest, discouraging and indifferent to her friends, the prisoner of her own unhappiness. And here was Charles, the only person she wanted — yet the most fateful events in both their lives had overtaken them while they were hundreds of miles apart. They were bound to feel strange.

Young Penny was disappointed at her father's unwarlike appearance. "I hoped you would be dressed like an Irishman, my lord."

"Did you, moppet? I'll try to bring you a real Irishman, a captive, next time I come."

"Will you? Is it a promise?" Both little girls gazed at him in adoration. Penny was nine, Isabel seven.

"Not a promise. But I'll do my best. You shall have the O'Neill, the mighty Earl of Tyrone himself, if I can catch him."

"When you do catch Tyrone," said Penelope, "you'll be required to bring his head on a charger. That's how Herodias likes her victims delivered."

Charles's lips narrowed in something very like disapproval.

"Herodias was a wicked queen in the Bible," Isabel informed them. "Madam, did you mean that our Queen . . . "

"Your mother meant nothing of the kind," said Charles hastily.

Oh, did I not? Penelope sopped the gravy with her manchet of bread. She said, "You haven't told me how you escaped from the old woman's clutches. Did she know you were coming to me?"

"I had Her Majesty's permission to inspect my estate."

Charles's manner was repressive, as his glance travelled from the children to the rank of attendants laden with plates and dishes. If he imagines the servants don't know how I feel, he's a simpleton, thought Penelope. She did not enjoy being snubbed.

Isabel had been pondering. She piped up. "My mother says the Queen is a murdering old witch . . . "

"You damned little liar! You never heard me say so!"

Penelope had caught something in Charles's expression that frightened her, so she frightened the child, who flooded into protesting tears.

"You did say it, madam! You did! When Lady Southampton was here . . . "

Penelope got up, pulled Isabel off her stool, and slapped her. "Haven't I told you enough times that I will not have back answers and impertinence? You'll go to your bed, Isabel, and you'll stay there for the rest of the day. We'll see if that will curb your taste for argument."

Isabel gulped, slithered from her mother's grasp, and rubbed her cheek. Poor little wretch, she was as white as a sheet. Penelope knew she was being brutally unjust, but she could not recant.

Charles had taken in this scene with only the faintest lift of an eyebrow. Now he reached out and drew his daughter into the shelter of his arm. She snuggled against him, her hair was exactly the same raven-black as his own; they were remarkably alike.

"You must not contradict your mother, Bel," he said. "Yet I think you meant no harm. Will your ladyship overlook her fault, this once? To celebrate my homecoming?"

Penelope was not sorry to have the sentence quashed. "Very well." She went back to her chair. "Since your father wishes it, Bel, you may stay. Go on with your dinner, and let us have some peace from your chatter."

"Yes, madam." And, with far more enthusiasm, "Your lordship is very kind to me; I wish you were always at home."

For the rest of the meal, Charles told stories about Ireland to amuse the children.

Afterwards he and Penelope went into

his bookroom, with its tall windows over the garden. She had so longed for the time when they would be alone, and now they seemed to have no common language.

She fidgeted about, shifting the ornaments. "I'm sorry I flew out at Bel; that girl would try the patience of a saint — which I am not. Now we've got rid of our daughters and our servants, am I allowed to speak frankly of the Queen?"

"If your frankness paints a portrait of Herodias, you had better get rid of me too." The tone was casual and ironic, but he added, "I mean that, Penelope."

"Well!" She stared at him. "You've got very dutiful since we last met. Is this the result of being her viceroy? You weren't always such a paragon."

"No need to remind me. When I came into her presence and remembered my effrontery — planning to make her my prisoner for what I thought was her own good — I tell you, Pen, I wanted to lie down like a dog and howl at her feet. But this I can claim: I have never spoken slightingly of her person or her character."

"I haven't your compunction. Not since she killed my brother."

"Penelope, she did not kill him," objected Charles. "He committed a crime for which the penalty is death. He was most scrupulously tried and convicted under English law. There was no doubt of his guilt — indeed, he confessed as much, and died penitent."

"Confessed!" The word was a running sore to her. "You know what Essex confessed, don't you? Nottingham sent you the gist of it. He tried to break your neck as well as mine."

Her anger swerved away from the Queen to Essex. Charles tried to reason with her.

"He may hardly have known what he was doing, his last few days on earth, and in such a pitiful case. We ought not to condemn him."

"Oh, you are too holy! You follow his fashion. Let's forget all our old ways, swallow every injury and grovel like a pack of canting Puritans!" She was losing her self-command, unleashing the fury caged up in a year of solitary brooding. Charles, the one person who ought to

337

have seen her point of view, had failed her. She had counted on Charles as an indignant partisan, and all she got was logic and preaching. It was the last straw. "I won't ask what you thought of my pious brother's choosing to inform the Privy Council that I was a strumpet. Your lordship doesn't resent that either, I take it?"

"Angel . . . "

"Don't you Angel me, Mountjoy! If you think I can be fobbed off with pet-names, just because you've made me your whore . . . "

"That's a filthy lie, and you know it!"

Charles covered the space between them in two long strides. He caught her by the arms, pinioning her elbows to her sides so roughly that she cried out from the pain. He was in a deadly, white-hot rage.

"How dare you cast such an accusation in my teeth, you damned little harpy? I haven't made you a whore. You are my wife, whether you believe it or not, and you will never speak to me in those terms again. For ten years I've given you my devoted love; I've done everything for you that lay within my power — and you would do well to remember it's your fault, not mine, that I couldn't do more."

She muttered something incoherent. The ruthless grip tightened.

"Stand still, do you hear me? And keep your mouth shut. You are going to attend to me for a change. I've always regarded you and treated you as my wife; if I have failed in my duty, it was from too much affection. I've been a great deal too easy with you, let you have your own way far too often. I dare say you think me a weakling. You are mistaken. I am very well able to rule you, Penelope."

She felt a shiver of apprehension run right through her body. The inexorable voice went on.

"You don't like to be ruled, do you? You won't bear the lightest touch of discipline. It suits you now to say that your brother and I, between us, have held you up to public scorn as my mistress, but you weren't so anxious, a year ago, to conduct yourself properly as my wife. You wanted the delights of love without the burden of obedience. I implored you to stop meddling with sedition; I hoped that for once in your life you might do as you

were told — but no! You had to embroil
yourself, you had to run round London,
hunting up more conspirators, like a
harlot soliciting custom, when anyone
with a grain of sense must have known
that hare-brained scheme was doomed
from the start. Poor Essex never could
plan a campaign . . . "

"It wasn't a hare-brained scheme!"

Charles had dealt such a series of
shattering blows to Penelope's self-esteem
that he had knocked the fight out of her,
but his last remark had touched a private
obsession which he had no means of
understanding, and which affected her so
deeply that everything else was forgotten.
She returned to the fray with a suddenly
renewed defiance.

"What do you know of the matter? You
weren't there. We were defeated, and we
paid for it — is it part of my punishment
that I have to listen to homilies from the
invincible Lord Deputy who can do no
wrong? I suppose you came back to me
out of pity. Well, I won't have your pity
at any price, and I won't have you either.
Get out of my sight — get out of this
house — I never want to see you again!"

Charles let go of her immediately, turned and left the room without a word.

"Charles, come back. I didn't mean it."

The words were not articulate until he had closed the door, and then it was too late. Penelope was alone in a wilderness of her own choosing, without any clear idea how she had got there. She was faced with the collapse of another relationship, and the searing pain of emotions wrenched into ugly and terrifying shapes, long-established harmony and trust shown up as a sham. What Robin had done to her, she and Charles had just done to each other, and she knew that she had caused most of the damage. She stumbled towards the nearest window-seat and crouched against it, in a spasm of dry, gasping sobs. Oh Charles, Charles, come back. I didn't mean it.

The house was very still; where was he? Suppose he had taken a horse and ridden straight off to the Court? No, he wouldn't abandon her; it couldn't end like this. But all she had been through with Robin had shaken her confidence, and she knew that directly Charles had stepped into the house there had been a latent antagonism between them. She had displeased him by abusing the Queen, and by being so unkind to poor little Isabel. I used not to be a bad mother, I've turned into a petulant shrew. No wonder he doesn't like what I am now; who would?

I'm still desirable, she told herself. But am I, to anyone so fastidious? After the way I acted today? He's had me for ten years; I'm older than he is, and women always lose, in that race. He's a young man still, and a famous man. There was that rumour Kate Howard passed on to me so agreeably: that he was to marry Ormonde's heiress and acquire vast property in Ireland. Isn't he entitled to forget our old promises now? When I accused him of treating me like a whore — how could I have said anything so wicked? Vast property and wealth, and a chaste little bride of sixteen; wouldn't he prefer that to a scold of thirty-eight who screams insults at him? How hideous I must have been. There's a hardness about me now, I know it. Soon I shall be refusing to look in the glass, like my

342

dear cousin Elizabeth. Perhaps I am like her; we both take after the Boleyns. Vain and coarse and spiteful; devils to our men. And they grow weary of such termagants, when the young lustre has worn off.

Savouring in advance all the humiliations of an ageing beauty, Penelope recognised a new factor which reduced her to panic. If Charles deserted her, she had absolutely nowhere to go. Discarded by Rich, banished from the Court, she had no status, no home, no money and four illegitimate children. In this utter penury, an echo from their quarrel came back to her. She had forgotten, after so many years, that Wanstead was no longer one of the family estates. She had excelled herself by ordering Charles out of his own house. Deflated egotism could sink no lower.

Someone had come into the bookroom. There were always servants about, tidying the cushions or making up the fire. Ignoring the movements behind her, she stared out of the window. It had begun to rain.

"Penelope."

Still sitting on the floor, she turned,

reluctant and defenceless. He was just inside the door. Across the length of the bookroom they measured each other.

And now she had a kind of revelation. In the first pleasure of his return, she had thought the Irish triumphs had not altered him. Perhaps there had been nothing to alter; the essential quality must always have been there, waiting to mature, but she had not perceived it. She had known him so long. The penniless boy, a servant in her stepfather's house, who had been sent away in disgrace for making love to her. The unknown law student who had come to Court when she was already a celebrity. The man who had got her with child, and was then obliged to rely on the Queen's favourite to save them both from the consequences. He had remained a part — though a very decorative and intelligent part — of the Devereux entourage, content to play second fiddle to his brilliant friend. Had she been treating Charles, all this time, with a complacent patronage? Certainly not in their private encounters as lovers, but in the outward give-and-take of every day? She knew now that the Lord Deputy of Ireland was a great man in his own right, with the originality, the tough and tireless strength of his particular genius. Besides which, she was being housed, fed and clothed at his expense. In future, any patronage would come from him.

The whole awareness of this, felt rather than reasoned, settled in one piece into her mind, while he was assessing her.

"If you are in a more rational frame of mind, I must speak with you."

"I am at your lordship's disposal."

It was an unfortunate phrase to have picked on, too near the literal truth. He would be giving the orders now; she would have to accept them with a good grace, and eat humble-pie. Because of her new sense of subjection and her dependence on his generosity but most of all because she needed his cherishing love so desperately that she would do anything to placate him. And surely he must know it.

If he did, he showed no sign of elation, but came towards her rather diffidently, saying, "Now we have both recovered our manners, I think we should cancel all grievances. Dear heart, don't think too ill of me. You got under my guard. I am too excessively in love with you — oh, my precious Angel!"

For she had scrambled to her feet and almost thrown herself into his arms, and they were kissing fervently, and breaking off to say how sorry they were, and each taking the blame. They had never had such a battle in the old days, and they never would again. Some lovers seemed to thrive on quarrelling; they must be mad.

"It's an odious pastime," she said. "Charles, I was vile to you. I knew that my horrible attack was false, even while I was making it. And as for ordering you out of your own house . . . "

"Yes, I wondered when you'd see the comedy in that."

"Comedy! If you knew how I have mortified myself in the past hour."

"My darling, there was no need. You may have fired the first shot, but I was so clumsy and impatient. I should have guessed how it still hurt you to speak of Essex."

Her regained happiness went out like a lamp.

"I can't even bear to think of him.

It's an unending torment. He hated me, Charles. He disowned me, at the end, and he died hating me."

"I'm sure that isn't true, sweetheart. He overcame all his demons, and died in a state of perfect charity."

"Oh yes, he prayed for his enemies," she said. "I was one of them."

Charles studied her thoughtfully, and took her to sit in the window-seat. He could tell there was something else she was trying to say, and being Charles, he waited, providing a haven of calm and safety.

At last she brought herself to the point, speaking very low, and looking away from him, out across the rain-washed terrace to the formal garden.

"I can't keep this to myself any longer. I can't face it alone. You know what he — Robin — said of me? That I urged him on continually, and told him that all his followers thought him a coward. I denied it to the Councillors, and I don't regret that; I'd do it again. Only — it was true, Charles. I did urge him, several times, to make up his mind one way or the other; I suppose my nagging seemed continual. And I did repeat those rumours that he'd lost his valour. I was so frightened by his melancholy; if you'd seen him in those moods — but that's no excuse. I was angry too. I lost my temper — my hellish temper again. Oh God, I wish I'd cut out my tongue!" She paused, bracing herself, "I can trust you, my lord. You've spoilt me with love, all these years; you won't spoil me with lies. Judge me. Did I send Robin to his death?"

He didn't hurry to reassure her, but considered the question with his usual air of detachment.

"No," he said at length. "I am certain you need not reproach yourself. Robert would not take up arms to refute an idle slander, however much it may have riled him. He became a rebel of his own free choice. Every action of his life was determined by his private judgment — that's why he got into such deep waters when his judgment betrayed him. No one, not even the Queen, ever succeeded in making Robert change his mind; you know that as well as I do. It's true he often asked advice — but only from the advisers he wanted to hear. Don't you recall how he behaved towards Cuffe? When he came out of prison, full of loyalty and high hopes, Cuffe was dismissed for preaching sedition. Then the Queen was unrelenting, so he called Cuffe back again to nourish his grievances. I dare say the things you told him may have served the same turn. But as to altering his purpose — no. You could no more have driven him on than Frank could hold him back. You didn't destroy him. He was the author of his own destruction ... Penelope, has this dread been weighing on you for a whole year?"

She nodded. Robin's describing her as an adulteress was a secondary evil which she had used as a hobby-horse. Behind it, never admitted in so many words but pursuing her night and day, was the monstrous fear that she was guilty of his death.

"My poor child," said Charles.

She was thirty-eight and he was six months younger. It did not feel like that, while she rested her head against his shoulder, as Isabel had done, and was wrapped in his gentle compassion. She had used most of his arguments to herself already, but they sounded far more convincing from the man whose clear-sighted integrity she respected so greatly. And confession was good for the soul — though it could be carried too far.

"What came over him in the Tower," she asked, "to cause that terrible remorse?"

"Surely the discovery that Cecil was innocent of treason, and that there was no reason whatever for a patriotic rising."

"He learnt that at his trial. It didn't affect him then."

"No, for it was sprung on him out of the blue. He had gone there prepared to fight for his reputation and to save Southampton if he could. I suppose he fought on by instinct. But afterwards, alone in his prison with only a few days to live, he must have started to think. I find no mystery in what followed."

She was not satisfied. "Why should he give way so completely? He knew all along that the rising was unlawful in itself, although his motive was good. Granted, he had misjudged Cecil, but an honest mistake . . . "

"It wasn't an honest mistake," said Charles. "Wait, love. I'm not implying that he invented those charges out of malice. He believed them with the surface of his mind. And he shouldn't have done. It came out that they were all based originally on one unsupported story that he had never troubled to check, though with his intelligence service he certainly had the means. The rumour begat others, as rumours do, when they find a fertile breeding-ground. He talked us all into accepting them, in that beguiling way he had; I was as bad as anyone, and I've been heartily sorry for it since. Once I got away from the faction, I began to exercise my wits. Cecil couldn't be a Spanish hireling. He didn't fit the part in any way. For one thing, he was too resolute over winning the war in Ireland — and the Catholic Irish are the natural allies of Spain. Then there was the other complaint: that he had gained too strong an ascendancy over the Queen. That was arrant nonsense. The Queen was still in sole command of her kingdom. I was made to feel the force of that from the moment she appointed me her viceroy. She didn't need rescuing, from her Secretary or anybody else. And Essex knew those two far better than I did. He had worked with them for years, in daily consultation. He was a man of great ability and wide experience, not ignorant or untaught. If he thought Cecil a Spanish agent and the Queen a silly old woman in her dotage, it could only be through wilful self-deception. Because that was what he wanted to think. That was his dishonesty."

She was both appalled and fascinated by this portrait. She had been slowly obliged to realise that there had been some fundamental flaw in Robin's nature; perhaps Charles could tell her what it was.

"You mean," she said, "that he had to believe the stories in order to justify his bid for power?"

"It was the only way. He could no longer hope to dominate through the Queen's favour. He couldn't succeed her, he wasn't royal. He wouldn't play the bold usurper, he was no Bolingbroke. He sacrificed the truth in exchange for these convenient fables. That was the price he was willing to pay, so that he could see himself as the national saviour."

Charles had always valued an absolute fidelity to the truth above all other virtues. Possibly he thought a self-deceiver more contemptible than an outright traitor. Not everyone could agree with that distinction.

"If he deluded himself," she said, "it was in a noble cause. All he ever wanted was to serve his country."

"There's a wealth of meaning in that 'all'. Essex used to say that he was not ambitious. In fact, he was the most ambitious man I ever met. He wanted nothing for his own advantage. He simply wanted the highest reward of a patriot: to know that he had performed greater services for England than any other living man. And that he demanded as a right. No one must surpass him, nothing must interfere with his dream. When things went wrong, he said the Queen was thwarting him; he would not admit that there might be impediments in his own nature, though he must have suspected — have you never fixed on the date when he began to change? When he became so obstinate and arrogant, far more inclined to quarrel with the Queen?"

"It was after the Islands Voyage." A clear pattern was emerging now. (If it be a sin to covet honour, I am the most offending soul alive.)

"Yes. That whole campaign was a disaster, and I believe that from then on he was plagued by a secret doubt of his own proficiency as a general. And this must have been intolerable, for it threatened the corner-stone of his delusion: that he was born to be a second Alexander. Unhappily he was nothing of the kind, which explains why he insisted on going to Ireland, and then behaved so strangely when he got there. He needed to prove himself by defeating Tyrone — yet he dared not put his fortune to the test, in case he failed. He took refuge in that ill-fated truce which brought about his eclipse; he could only get back into power by making a scapegoat of Cecil, and that led him finally into rebellion. What a damnable, tragic waste! He wasn't a villain. He wanted to give his whole life to the service of England. The trouble was that he wanted to give more than he

354

possessed. He aspired to a destiny which God did not intend for him; I suppose that must be accounted a sin of pride in its most exalted form. And there's no other sin that exacts so heavy a penalty. It's not for us to condemn him, but can you not see how a man such as Robert would condemn himself if his eyes were suddenly opened?"

Charles must have been working this out with much deliberation during the lonely months in Ireland. Had he arrived at the truth which had come to Robin in the Tower? It was a desolating verdict, yet what else could explain the moral collapse, the self-disgust, the abject desire for punishment and death?

"It's terrible to think of," she whispered. "If he saw himself as you do, not only a traitor, but vain, besotted, presumptuous. What can such a revelation have done to him?"

"I think it broke his heart," said Charles.

Robin, my dear, no wonder you wanted to die.

"Where did he go astray?" she asked, after a pause. "He was always so good as a boy, more fit for the Church than the Court. There was no taint of false pride or arrogance. People are saying now that he was spoilt by success, but it wasn't apparent at the height of his fame."

"No. There you have the whole paradox. He was amazingly gifted in so many ways, yet the most notable thing about him was his heart-warming generosity and candour. He was chivalrous, honest and loyal. He disarmed envy. In the light of his own character, his gifts shone doubly bright. Everyone loved him and delighted to praise him, some to the verge of idolatry. I suppose that was where the danger lay. If ever a man might be excused for thinking a little too well of himself, that man was Essex.

"I believe," added Charles soberly, "that we were partly to blame for rating his abilities somewhat higher than they deserved. Because we loved him, it was easy to feel that what he obtained by favour had been won by merit. We certainly encouraged him to think so. And it's all very well to speak of presumption, but when a man is made a Knight of the Garter at twenty-one, and a Privy Councillor at twenty-five, what limits can you expect him to set himself at thirty?"

"Well, you know where to go for an answer to that question," retorted Penelope with a sudden venom. "You know who it was that praised and idolised more lavishly than all the rest, corrupted him and then cast him out. According to your reckoning, she was the true author of his destruction. Can you still defend her?"

"No one can defend her. Good God, Penelope, do you think she tries to defend herself? Do you think she doesn't know what she has done? All through indulging a handsome, eager boy, advancing him too early and perhaps too far. I don't suppose that unhappy woman has had one hour free from suffering since she signed the warrant. Nor ever will again. My darling, you hate her, here in exile, but if you could see her now I'm sure you would be moved to pity. They say she can't sleep. That she shuts herself up in the dark and weeps for him."

Penelope made no comment.

"You must try to forgive her," he said.

"You must try to forgive them both. Not for their sake; there is no harm you can do to either of them now. But for your own. You will never have any peace until you do."

He held her hands in the long silence.

"I'll try," she said at last. "If it's what you want, Charles. But it won't be easy. You'll have to help me."

She would need help in learning to forgive the Queen. As for Robin, that struggle was already over. Charles had drawn out the poison that had been festering ever since she read that painful confession. He had made her look beyond herself to imagine Robin's state of mind as he wrote, in his dark night of despair, deeply contrite and ashamed. Perhaps he had not hated her, after all. Perhaps his love for her had made it necessary for him to include her in his total rejection of everything that had once seemed precious. None of the sins he had ascribed to her and Charles could lighten the weight of guilt he had acknowledged himself.

"'O God, be merciful unto me,' he had said on the scaffold, 'the most wretched creature on earth.'"

358

She began to cry, but softly and freely, expressing a natural grief. This was quite different from the agonies of self-accusing horror that had racked her for the past year. Now she wept simply for the loss of a dear brother, loving him without resentment, as she had not been able to do since the day of his execution.

And this time Charles was there to comfort her.

3

IT rained all night; Penelope said Charles had brought his weather with him. The wind lamenting in the trees merely increased the sense of warmth and peace indoors. And next morning the sun shone and the world sparkled.

Charles and Penelope walked in the garden, inspecting the delicate shoots that were just breaking through the March soil, the ornamental conceits and devices, gay in their coat of spring paint, the paths of coloured sand and crushed shells. In the wilderness they heard the children calling to each other. Mount, grubbing under a bank, had found a nesting hedgehog. And all the grass from the fishpond to the orchard was starred with gold: sweep after sweep of lent lilies unfolding their trumpets to the light.

Charles, the inveterate gardener, was busy planning improvements.

"We must have that old apple tree down. And cut back the holly hedge, it throws too much shade. Don't you think so, love?"

Penelope agreed. She would have agreed with anything he said, in a mood of serenity that was worlds away from yesterday's bitterness. Charles had worked this miracle, by disentangling her helpless misery, and by being there to cherish and comfort her. It doesn't suit me to live without a man, she thought.

Or rather, it did not suit her to live without Charles. No one else had been able to make her happy. She had never been entirely unfaithful to her first love, even during the years when they had apparently forgotten each other. Philip Sidney had once possessed her heart, and Rich had possessed her body, but Charles was the only man to whom she had ever given both. It was twenty-two years since they had slipped out to their secret meetings in this garden, a boy and girl with no premonition of what fate had in store for them. And here they were, after many separations and vicissitudes, held together by a love whose intensity and richness would have seemed unattainable to most couples of nearly forty, if not downright indecorous.

Where was that love going to take them next, she wondered.

"You hope to be recalled," she said, "as soon as you've hunted down Tyrone. What then? Am I to live with you here? You're a great man now, Charles. It's certain the Queen will make you a Councillor, probably Master of the Ordnance as well. I don't want the scandal of my presence to cast a blight on your glory."

"My glory will be worth very little without your presence. And I doubt if anyone will care, they're used to us by now. I want you to stay with me, Angel. Under my roof and in my bed. I'm tired of trafficking between your house and mine at four in the morning, it's too cold — and quite unbecoming to a Privy Councillor. I must study to be dignified."

Penelope laughed. He was looking particularly urbane, the model of a distinguished nobleman. She found his ideas of dignity refreshing.

"What's more," he said, "if we come out into the open, Rich may be goaded

362

into divorcing you. Then we can have a wedding in church with all the ceremonies."

Penelope had begun to pick a bunch of lent lilies. She straightened up, feeling slightly dizzy.

"Dear heart, what are you talking about? Rich can't sue for an annulment, any more than I can. And if he divorced me for adultery, I should be forbidden to marry again. We can't get round that."

"I'm not so sure. There are special circumstances. Quite apart from the fact that you were contracted to me before Rich ever came on the scene — we shall never prove that now, so it's not worth trying. But there are other reasons. You were bullied into accepting Rich under duress, you protested your unwillingness at the altar; plenty of people would say that rendered the marriage invalid. And there's talk of altering the Canon Law so that a divorce can be granted on the grounds of 'deadly hostility', both parties being free to marry again; Luther considered that permissible, so did Calvin, and I can't think of any hostility more deadly than that brute has shown towards you. Even while the law remains unchanged, there are members of the clergy who would see your case in that light. If once you were divorced, for whatever cause, I'm certain I could find a parson whose conscience would allow him to marry us. I dare say we should raise a storm of disapproval from the Bishops, in fact we might cause a greater scandal than we have already. Does that thought deter you?"

Penelope said she had ridden out so many storms, one more wouldn't sink her. She stood gazing across the green slope to the forest, absently crushing the stalks of the daffodils; their sticky juice ran down her fingers.

"Charles, why do you want to do this? You've always maintained that we are married in the sight of God . . . "

"And you've never entirely agreed with me."

She was stricken by compunction. She had struggled to hide her occasional fits of guilt, she did not see why he should be called on to respect them, for she had certainly not allowed them to interfere with her pleasure.

364

"My darling, I don't know what I believe. My theology isn't as clear as yours. One thing I know for certain, no woman ever had a better husband, and if I have seemed grudging and ungrateful . . . " A distressing thought occurred to her. "Are you brooding over the infamous way I attacked you yesterday? Can't you forgive me and forget it?"

"I've done both already," he said promptly. "We forgave each other, didn't we, for all the cruel cuts that drew blood yesterday? Why, sweetheart, there's no need for so many heart-searchings. It's true that I think our present state is perfectly lawful, and that we don't require any form of ritual to absolve us, but surely you can understand that I should like to take you to church and get our marriage blessed? And it's the only way I can publicly acknowledge you as my wife. It grates on my ear that you still have to be called Lady Rich. I have an overwhelming ambition to hear you addressed as Lady Mountjoy."

He gave her a sideways glance, full of self-mockery, as though he was inviting her to laugh at him. At the same time she had an impression that the fulfilment of this dream would mean more to him than any of his other achievements.

Echoing his manner, she said lightly, "You couldn't welcome the change more gladly than I should. I'm sick of being saddled with the dubious honours of the rich Lord Rich. I should so much prefer to be a Blount."

It was no good building too much on the prospect, for the chances were still very remote. They strolled on, arm in arm, and got a glimpse of Penny, carefully carrying a bowl of milk for the hedgehog, with Mount trotting beside her.

"There's nothing we can do," said Penelope regretfully, "to make the children legitimate."

"No. But we might render their station more honourable."

One other matter remained to be dealt with, she had been thinking it over seriously before he distracted her with this new possibility.

"Whether or not we can ever be married in church, we must continue together as husband and wife."

"It's rather late to consider any other

366

arrangement." He sounded amused.

"A plague on you, Charles! Has your mind no furniture except a bed? Now you've made me forget what I was going to say." She stood still collecting her wits and started again, with a certain stiffness.

"I have it on my conscience that I have not always behaved to you as I should. I expected you to treat me as your wife, and then refused to observe my side of the bargain, I wanted to eat my cake and keep my freedom. I know I have done wrong, and I'm very sorry for it, and for the times when I've been unbiddable — and disobedient. From now on, my lord, I promise to submit to your authority — at least, I'll try," she added frankly, aware of her limitations. "And this is because it ought to be so, and not because you are paying for every crust I eat."

She caught a flicker of surprise in his face, and then an expression she had never seen before. He looked like a man whose ship was coming into harbour after a long voyage.

"You did not have to give me that assurance," he said slowly. "And the

367

crusts are neither here nor there. But I know how to value such a promise, even though I may never hold you to it. You won't find me a tyrant, Penelope."

No one could be less tyrannical. She was on very safe ground; they might never have another serious clash of wills. If they did, she would give way and do as she was told. Nothing less would satisfy the feeling she had for him now.

They crossed the great avenue of beech-trees which led from the main gate in a straight line to the house. How often she had ridden along this avenue with Robin, coming from the Court; how happy he had always been at the first sight of his home. Robin's image was everywhere at Wanstead. For a year she had been trying to ignore it. She would not try any longer; that was no way to treat the memory of a hero, it was not the way the rest of his countrymen were treating him. For he had been a national hero, in spite of everything, and his fame still burnt clear. Charles had remarked last night, with his usual generosity, that Cadiz would be remembered after Kinsale was forgotten, and he was probably right:

Cadiz had been the outstanding victory of their generation. Charles had also told her that Robin's Garter banner was still hanging in St. George's Chapel at Windsor; the Queen had ordered that it should remain there as a tribute to his many years of great and valiant service to the Crown. Penelope had bitten back a sharp comment, and then found in herself a faint stirring of charity towards the Queen.

Everything was coming into a different perspective, even the fact that Robin had sunk to the depths of writing that terrible confession. She had seen it originally as an act of contemptible cowardice and self-betrayal; now she was beginning to wonder if it was the bravest thing he had ever done. After blinding himself for so long with the dazzling vision of his own righteousness, how much easier it would have been to go on hugging his illusions, justifying his mistakes, so that he could have the consolation of believing himself a patriotic martyr. Instead of which, be had finally faced the humiliating truth, at the eleventh hour and in great tribulation, rejecting every scrap of pride or comfort, because he saw in that total surrender his only hope of making his peace with God. He had wanted the Queen's forgiveness, but not with any idea of escaping the consequences of what he had done; it was remorse that had defeated him, not fear. Isolated and wretched, utterly broken in spirit, he had managed to die like a soldier, with impeccable courage and fortitude, strengthened by the one support that had been left to him when everything else was lost: the hard, bare rock of his faith. And that was the one thing that counted in the end.

No, she would never again think that there was any disgrace in the way that Robin had met his death.

Charles had made it possible for her to recognise this. He was not only giving her the future, he had given her back the past as well, each a necessary complement to the other. In Charles's company — perhaps eventually as his acknowledged wife — she would be able to go on living. To heal the wounds in her mind that had nearly crippled her. To be thankful that life still had so much good in it. Even to think of Robin without pain.

Author's Note

All the characters in this novel are drawn from history. Readers may be interested to know what happened to Penelope and her family after the end of the story.

Mountjoy, the greatest English soldier of his day, finally defeated Tyrone and brought him to Wanstead as a prisoner, early in 1603, to make his submission to the new King. James I showered rewards on the victorious general, who was created Earl of Devonshire and became one of the most influential men in the country. The King and Queen also showed great favour to Penelope, who was made a peeress in her own right, in the style of 'the ancientest Earls of Essex, called Bourchier, whose heir her father was'. She and Charles were now living together quite openly in a blaze of honours and splendour.

In 1605 Lord Rich obtained a divorce from Penelope, and on the 20th December she was married to Charles Blount, Earl of Devonshire, in the private chapel at Wanstead by his domestic chaplain, William Laud, afterwards Archbishop of Canterbury. This provoked an uproar which involved them all, Laud saying sadly that the Earl of Devon's marriage was his cross. There had been certain alterations to the Canon Law in 1603, but no concessions on the subject of divorce. The King had condoned the association while the couple were ostensibly 'living in sin'. After the religious ceremony, which they sincerely believed to be valid, he banished them from the Court.

Devonshire was extremely indignant. He wrote a vehement letter to the King, defending Penelope, and insisting that there was 'nothing unscriptural in her behaviour nor aught contrary to the Canon Law.' He based his argument chiefly on the fact that she had been coerced into marrying Rich against her will. It is impossible to say how this controversy would have ended, for in March Devonshire was suddenly taken ill. He died ten days later, on the 3rd April, 1606.

Penelope died the following year, at the age of forty-four. She was received into the Roman Catholic Church on her deathbed.

Penelope left ten children, five Riches and five Blounts. (The Dictionary of National Biography gives the number as twelve; this is because the two Blount daughters appear in the Rich family tree. To add to the confusion, there were two sons called Charles, one by each father.) Devonshire's will, signed the day before his death, definitely acknowledged which of the children were his: Mountjoy, St. John, Charles, Penelope, Isabel, 'and the child the lady now goeth withal'.

This last child may have miscarried. The other ten all grew up. Three of the sons became earls. Robert Rich succeeded his father, who had been made Earl of Warwick. Henry Rich was created Earl of Holland. These two brothers, like their cousin, the third Earl of Essex, fought for the Parliament in the Civil War. Mountjoy Blount, being illegitimate, could not inherit his father's titles, which became extinct, but he was created Baron Mountjoy in his own right, and later Earl of Newport. He fought in the Civil War as a Royalist.

Frances, Countess of Essex, married again in 1603. Her third husband was the Irish Earl of Clanrickarde who, as Lord Dunkellin, had been a friend of both Essex and Mountjoy. This marriage lasted nearly thirty years.

Some readers may wonder why I have ignored the legend of the Queen's Ring, which is the one anecdote everyone has heard about Essex. I believe this was a myth concocted by the Jacobean public, who revered both Essex and the Queen, and wanted a scapegoat to blame for his tragic death. All the evidence refutes the idea that he appealed secretly to the Queen for mercy. In the very full accounts of his last fortnight there is not the smallest suggestion that he either expected or wished to survive. Quite the reverse. At his trial, when he was still playing the part of an injured patriot, he made no attempt to save himself, and after his breakdown in the Tower he longed for death as his only means of expiation. This would not have seemed morbid to an Elizabethan — though it is clear that Essex was emotionally unstable, to say the least. He was also a far more gifted, sympathetic and complex character than some modern writers make him out. All the good qualities I have given him are recorded by his contemporaries or revealed in his charming letters. His effect on those who knew him was extraordinary.

Essex and Mountjoy each had observant secretaries who left many details of their personal manners and idiosyncrasies.

The nicknames I have used are genuine. Essex was Robin to his family, he called his wife Frank, and Penelope was Mountjoy's Angel.

Other titles in the
Ulverscroft Large Print Series:

TO FIGHT THE WILD
Rod Ansell and Rachel Percy

Lost in uncharted Australian bush, Rod Ansell survived by hunting and trapping wild animals, improvising shelter and using all the bushman's skills he knew.

COROMANDEL
Pat Barr

India in the 1830s is a hot, uncomfortable place, where the East India Company still rules. Amelia and her new husband find themselves caught up in the animosities which seethe between the old order and the new.

THE SMALL PARTY
Lillian Beckwith

A frightening journey to safety begins for Ruth and her small party as their island is caught up in the dangers of armed insurrection.

THE SONG OF THE PINES
Christina Green

Taken to a Greek island as substitute for David Nicholas's secretary, Annie quickly falls prey to the island's charms and to the charms of both Marcus, the Greek, and David himself.

GOODBYE DOCTOR GARLAND
Marjorie Harte

The story of a woman doctor who gave too much to her profession and almost lost her personal happiness.

DIGBY
Pamela Hill

Welcomed at courts throughout Europe, Kenelm Digby was the particular favourite of the Queen of France, who wanted him to be her lover, but the beautiful Venetia was the mainspring of his life.

FATAL RING OF LIGHT
Helen Eastwood

Katy's brother was supposed to have died in 1897 but a scrawled note in his handwriting showed July 1899. What had happened to him in those two years? Katy was determined to help him.

NIGHT ACTION
Alan Evans

Captain David Brent sails at dead of night to the German occupied Normandy town of St. Jean on a mission which will stretch loyalty and ingenuity to its limits, and beyond.

A MURDER TOO MANY
Elizabeth Ferrars

Many, including the murdered man's widow, believed the wrong man had been convicted. The further murder of a key witness in the earlier case convinced Basnett that the seemingly unrelated deaths were linked.